THE UGLIEST HOUSE IN THE WORLD

Peter Ho Davies was born in 1966, to Welsh and Chinese parents, grew up in Coventry, and now divides his time between Britain and the US, where he teaches at the University of Michigan. His prize-winning stories have appeared in many magazines and anthologies, including *Critical Quarterly*, *Paris Review*, and *The Best American Short Stories*, and his second short-story collection, *Equal Love*, will be published by Granta Books in 2000.

THE UGLIEST HOUSE IN THE WORLD

STORIES

PETER HO DAVIES

Granta Books
London

Granta Publications, 2/3 Hanover Yard, London N1 8BE

First published in Great Britain by Granta Books 1998
This edition published by Granta Books 1999

The following stories appeared in slightly different form in these publications: 'The Ugliest House in the World' in *Antioch Review*, *Critical Quarterly* and *The Best American Short Stories 1995;* 'Relief' in *The Paris Review;* 'Safe' in *Agni;* 'I Don't Know, What Do You Think?' in *The Greensboro Review;* 'Buoyancy' in *Story;* 'The Silver Screen' in *Harvard Review* and *The Best American Short Stories 1996.*

A CIP catalogue record for this book is available from the British Library

1 3 5 7 9 10 8 6 4 2

Typeset by M Rules
Printed and bound in Great Britain by
Mackays of Chatham plc

For my parents

ACKNOWLEDGMENTS

Thanks are due to everyone who has read and commented on these stories but especially to Lynne Raughley, Marshall N. Klimasewiski, Fred Leebron, Kathryn Rhett, and Janet Silver. I am also grateful to the Henfield Foundation and the Fine Arts Work Center in Provincetown for their generous support during the writing of this book.

A number of sources were helpful for the historical stories in this collection, but the following books and their authors proved especially valuable: *The Washing of the Spears*, by Donald R. Morris; *The North Wales Quarrymen 1874–1922*, by R. Merfyn Jones; *In Patagonia*, by Bruce Chatwin; and *The War of the Running Dogs*, by Noel Barber. Any inaccuracies are my responsibility, as, of course, are the occasional historical liberties I've taken.

"Use every man after his desert,
and who shall 'scape whipping?"

Hamlet II, ii

CONTENTS

THE UGLIEST HOUSE IN THE WORLD

ASH CASH

Rellies are relatives. Grumblies are patients. Gerries are geriatrics. Ash cash is the money you get when you sign a cremation form.

A full house is when someone comes into Accident and Emergency with every bone in their arms and legs broken. I once saw a woman with a full house. She'd been fighting with her husband in the car and told him to stop. When he wouldn't, she opened the door and jumped out.

Accident and Emergency is called A&E. I did my last job in A&E, but I couldn't afford it, so now I'm working on a gerry ward. Gerries are the grumbliest grumblies of them all, but the ash cash from a job on gerries keeps me in food and drink all week, which means I can keep up the payments on my student loan. You don't get any money when they bury a patient, because if they have any doubts about the cause of death they can dig the body up again. But with cremation someone has to take responsibility. That's what they pay you for. Fortunately, cremation is more popular with gerries by a ratio of three to one.

A taff is a Welshman. Everyone in the doctors' mess calls me taff or taffy. Mr. Swain, the mortuary attendant, calls me boyo, especially during the rugby season when Wales lose badly. Last winter when Wales were touring Australia and losing each game by world-record scores, I'd order a lager in the mess and everyone would shout, "Make mine a Fosters, mate." Once, Mr. Swain actually welcomed me into the morgue wearing a bush hat with corks dangling around the rim. Last winter I had to visit the mortuary on an almost daily basis to fill out crem forms.

I'm not really Welsh. I don't speak Welsh. I've never lived in Wales. But my father is Welsh, and since he was laid off last year he's moved back there and bought a cottage with his golden handshake. He was fulfilling a promise he made to himself when my mother died. The cottage was three miles from the place he was born and ten miles from the chapel where they married. When I said I wasn't happy about it and that I'd been hoping to see more of him, he said, "It can't be helped. I've been promising myself this for twelve years. It's not as if you haven't had warning. I always kept my promises to you. Now I'm going to keep one to myself."

A golden handshake is what they give you when you've been working for the same company for thirty-five years and they lay you off with a month's notice and before your pension comes due. "Golden handshake!" he said. "Makes me feel like King Midas." My father's handshake was worth twenty-five thousand pounds, and he spent it all on his cottage. I told him he could have had it for less.

"What about the Welsh nationalists?" I said. "What if they start another arson campaign against holiday homes?"

"So?" he said. "I'm not a tourist. This is my home."

"But what if you want to sell? This is a holiday home. It's too small for a family. You could only ever sell it to tourists. If they start burning cottages again you'll never get twenty-five thousand back for it."

"I won't be selling," he said. "This is my home. This is where I plan to live from now on."

He certainly could have had the cottage for less, but he liked the idea of spending the whole sum on it. He liked the neatness of that. I think he could have knocked them down a couple of thousand on what they were asking. A couple of thousand would pay off about half my debt. A couple of thousand is about six months of ash cash on gerries, and about a year on any other ward.

When I go into the morgue to sign the form for Mrs. Patel, Mr. Swain is there as usual, sitting at his desk in the bright windowless room. He's reading a thing in the paper about Neil Kinnock, the leader of the Labour party and a Welshman. "Dr. Williams," he calls out when he sees me. "Have you read this?"

"I don't have time to read papers, Mr. Swain."

"It says here that if Kinno wins the election he's going to do to the country what your people have been doing to sheep for centuries."

Mrs. Patel is so pale I hardly recognize her. She'd been one of our best patients — quiet, clean, and uncomplaining. The staff would have been quite sorry to lose her if it wasn't for her rellies, who were so demanding and suspicious of the hospital that everyone was glad to see the back of them. I sign the form and hand it to Swain.

"I hope you don't mind a joke, doctor," he says as he passes the receipt across.

"No," I say. "As a matter of fact, I'm going to Wales this weekend."

"Ah, a romantic getaway?"

"A funeral."

And Swain, who lays out bodies every day and talks to them and reads to them from his paper, blushes. The roll of fat at his neck goes bright red against the collar of his white coat.

"I'm so sorry," he says.

MY FATHER FISHES WITH HIS BARE HANDS

On the morning of the funeral, I look out the window of my father's cottage and see him up to his ankles in the waters of the stream. He is crouching over rocks and encircling them in his arms. From this distance it looks as if he is trying to get a grip and heave them out of the streambed, but I know he's just running his fingers around them, feeling for trout. I watch him for ten minutes as he moves from rock to rock, wading unsteadily through the water. Then I pull an anorak over my robe and push my bare feet into my shoes and go out to fetch him.

He calls it trout tickling. It's an old poacher's method.

"No rod, no line, no hooks, no nets. No incriminating evidence," as he says.

I don't want to go all the way down the field, but I don't want to shout to him. It's too early and I don't want to hear my voice ringing off the stone walls and slate roofs of the village. Besides, he'll accuse me of scaring off the fish. Everything I do always scares off the fish. Standing on the bank, my shadow on the water scares them off. Running beside the stream as a child, my footsteps scared them off. Little grains of earth rolled down the bank and alerted them. "My setting foot in Wales scares them off," I tell him.

"You'll catch your death," he says when I get close. He doesn't turn round. He has his head cocked, looking away into the distance, concentrating on his fingertips under the surface. I look at his feet in the water. They are so white they shine. I wonder what kind of feeling he can have in his fingers. He closes his hands and draws them out empty and dripping.

"Look who's talking. You better come in. It's time to get ready."

"Another ten minutes," he says. "You used to be able to pull them out of here in a bucket. But I know there's at least one bugger left. I saw him with the boy."

He looks back at the stream, choosing another rock.

"Come on. I'm freezing my bollocks off here." He begins to bend down. I look around and go over to the nearest molehill and scoop up two handfuls of loose earth and throw them in the water upstream from him.

"What the bloody hell are you doing?"

"Out," I say. "Now." I clap my hands together and the dirt flies off them.

"You're worse than your mother," he says, but he wades to the bank and I give him my hand.

"You're a sight." Standing on the bank with his old trousers rolled up past his knees and his shirtsleeves pushed up past his elbows, he looks like a child who's grown out of his clothes.

"You can talk," he says. I pass him his shoes and socks and let him lean on my shoulder to pull them on. I put an arm round his waist to steady him, but he shakes it off.

"I can manage."

"Fine."

I don't want to start anything this morning. Last night, I arrived and heard the kettle whistling from the street. When I went inside it was glowing red-hot and the whole cottage was full of steam. I ran through all the rooms thinking he'd had a stroke, and then I found him sitting on the wall out back looking down toward the stream. "It's only a kettle," he said innocently, and I said, "The last time it was only a microwave."

I start back toward the cottage, picking my way around the piles of sheep droppings scattered everywhere. "I'll never understand why you let their sheep in here. We could repair the wall in an afternoon."

"They keep the grass down."

"They fertilize it so it grows more. Sheep aren't as dumb as they look."

"Your grandmother used to pick up horse droppings

in her handkerchief and bring them back in her handbag for her roses."

I stop and put my arm on his shoulder. "Don't give yourself any ideas."

THE UGLIEST HOUSE IN THE WORLD

THE UGLIEST HOUSE IN THE WORLD — 100 YARDS is a sign on the road just before you reach my father's village. The story of the ugliest house is that there was once a law in Wales that if you could build a house in a day and sleep a night in it, an acre of land around it was yours. The house had to be stone just to make things a little harder. That's why the ugliest house is so ugly. It's little more than eight feet high, with higgledy-piggledy walls of granite and slate. The walls were originally drystone, which means they were built without cement. Rocks were just balanced one upon the other, with smaller stones wedged between them to stop them rocking.

Six years ago, Mr. Watkins, the farmer who owns the ugliest house, decided to open it to the public in the hope that he could make some money from tourists. The name came from his daughter, Kate. She called it that when she was a little girl. The farmer had to pay to put a new corrugated iron roof on it, and the council made him pour wavy lines of concrete between some of the looser rocks. The effect was to make the house even uglier.

There is a plaque inside and a single light bulb by which to read it, since the ugliest house has only one small window. The plaque tells the story with a few embellishments. No one actually lived there except for that one night required by law. The family who built the place had a perfectly good home in the village and they just wanted the land for grazing. In bad weather their sheep were penned in the house. Between the wars it was used as a shelter for tramps, and the plaque mentions a rumor that George Orwell spent a night there researching *Down and Out in Paris and London*. Since then, the house has been a shelter for climbers in the area and then from 1955 to 1966 a bus shelter for the White Star line.

Farmer Watkins hoped that the ugliest house would provide an income for Kate when she came back from Liverpool, pregnant at the age of sixteen. She learned the plaque off by heart and sat at the door with her child for a whole summer to charge admission, but the takings from that first season weren't even enough to pay for the roof. The farmer made one last attempt to have HOME OF THE UGLIEST HOUSE IN THE WORLD added to the name signs at either end of the village, but the council refused to even put it to a vote.

Mr. Watkins stood up in the meeting and shouted, "Fascists! Communists! Tin-pot dictators!" But the leader of the council shouted him down: "This meeting does not have time for frivolous notions and will eject any time-wasters from these proceedings. Sit down, Emlyn, you bloody idiot." Kate went to a technical college in Caernarfon instead, and learned hairdressing, and Mr. Watkins abandoned his front room to the smells of ammonia and peroxide.

The Watkinses are my father's nearest neighbors. Their farm has several acres of land turned over to sheep. The ugliest house lies between the two properties and they share the stream in which my father fishes. The name of the village is Carmel and on the hillside above it are others called Bethel and Bethesda — all named from the Old Testament.

THE SECOND UGLIEST HOUSE IN THE WORLD

Before walking up the street to the chapel, I polish my father's black shoes and help him on with them. His feet in his socks are as cold and smooth as stone and I rub them hard before I slip the shoes on. They feel like they've been worn down by the stream. He sips his tea and looks out the window while I rub. Afterwards, he looks at himself in the mirror while I brush the dandruff off his shoulders.

When we step outside, I can see mourners emerging from all the houses of the village, making their way to the chapel. Kate and her father are being helped up their path and I tell Father to wait. We hang around in front of the cottage, stamping our feet and blowing on our hands.

I call my father's cottage the second ugliest house in the world. Inside it is bright and cozy, but outside it is finished in pebble dash. Pebble dash is a traditional style of decoration in North Wales. It is literally what it says it is. When the plaster on the outside walls is still wet, handfuls of tiny pebbles — gravel, really — are thrown at it. I suppose it gives added insulation. In general, the style calls for the walls to be whitewashed and then the effect can be quite pleasing. Unfortunately, the tourists who owned the house before my father had the bright idea of redoing the pebble dash with multicoloured gravel like you find at the bottom of fish tanks. They let the field grow over with heather and long grass, and the moles undermine it; they let the boundary walls collapse and the gate rust; but they did over the house.

Every time I visit my father, I offer to whitewash the whole house. He always says, "I'll get to it. What's the rush? I'm a retired gentleman now." Since I found out he was living off sausages and baked beans I always bring a couple of bags of groceries when I come to visit him, but once I set four tins of paint on the kitchen table. He got angry and said, "I'll do it. I don't need your bloody help. Your heart's not in it anyway."

He means that I don't approve of his moving here. He's right.

"Why do you come, then?" he asks me whenever I bring it up.

"Because I want to spend some time with you. Is that a crime?"

Kate says it best. "The average age in North Wales is fifty-three. Unemployment is at twenty-nine percent. The population has fallen faster than the population of any other region in Britain in the last ten years." Kate puts copies of the *Economist* and the *New Statesman* on the table in her kitchen when she wants to turn it into a waiting room for her customers. She offered a skinhead cut, dyed red at half-price during the last election. She charges girls to pierce their ears, but she offers one free ear to boys. She calls Wales "the land of the dead, an old folks' home the size of a country."

Kate hates it here. She tells me how much she envies my life. "Why?" I say. "Because you're not stuck here," she says. "You're not stuck," I tell her. "Oh no," she says. "Not at all. A twenty-two-year-old hairdresser with a six-year-old son. I'm very mobile. I'm so light and flighty I'm surprised I don't just float away."

Gareth, Kate's son, had a lot to do with the success of her business. The old ladies who came to her most often never opened one of her magazines. They spent all their time gazing at Gareth. They used to leave a separate little something for him after they'd tip Kate.

IAN RUSH WALKS ON WATER

Gareth was a six-year-old Liverpool fan when my father moved in next to the ugliest house in the world. He wore his red team shirt everywhere, and when Kate wanted it to wash, he kept pestering her for the away-team strip. In the end, his grandfather bought it for him. "Forty quid those shirts cost," Kate told me. "And he grows out of them every year. We spoil him rotten."

Kate hated that Gareth was a Liverpool fan. It reminded her of his father. "He was a wanker," she told me once. "But he was a way out of this dump. I wouldn't have minded if he'd just left me. I could have made do. I could have found someone else. But when he left me with Gareth, where else could I go?"

Gareth and my father used to play football in the garden of the cottage. They moved two rocks from the top of the drystone wall marking the boundary between the two properties and used them for goal posts. I used to watch them, sometimes with Kate. Gareth was too small to shoot from a long way out. He had to get close to the goal before he could kick the ball far enough to take a shot, but then my father would come charging out like an old bear and bundle him over and take the ball. He'd hold him off with one arm until Gareth got tired trying to run around him. They would both be laughing and panting. When the boy began to hack his shins my father would drop-kick the ball into a far corner of the field. He used to find that funny. He didn't like it when I called him a cheat. "If I didn't cheat," he said, "I couldn't play with him."

"He loves you," Kate said.

"Did you use to cheat like that when you played with me?"

"I honestly can't remember."

"As your doctor, I'm telling you, you should take it easy out there."

As Gareth got closer you could always hear him talking to himself breathlessly. At first it was just mumbling, but as he got closer you would hear this running commentary on his own game: "He passes to Rush. Rush beats one man. He beats two. Still Rush. He turns. Shoots. Scores!"

Ian Rush is Liverpool's star striker and a Welshman.

Kate told me that Gareth was once sent home from Sunday school for carving graffiti into the desks. He carved "Liverpool AFC" and "You'll never walk alone" and "Ian Rush walks on water."

I was a big disappointment to Gareth, I think. He would run up to me where I leaned on the gate with his mother and try to pull me away.

"Why don't you play?" he'd ask.

"I don't think so, Gareth. I've got a bad ankle."

"But you're a doctor."

"Doctors get hurt too."

"But you can make yourself better."

"I'm on holiday. I don't even make myself better on holiday."

Another time he said to me, "Why don't you live here? Your dad lives here. If you lived here your ankle might get better and you could play football with us."

Another time he said, "If you had a little boy he'd want you to play with him."

"Gareth, I'm not even married."

"So? Do you have a girlfriend?"

"Gareth, don't you have anyone your own age to play with?"

"No."

The first time I met Gareth, he scored a goal and threw himself to his knees the way he had seen the players do on TV. Unfortunately, my father's field wasn't Anfield and he slid into a half-buried rock. He began to wail. His mother came rushing out of their house, and my father ran to the boy.

"It's okay," my father kept saying.

"What happened?" Kate said.

They called me to have a look at him, but I just smiled and waved. My father came over.

"What's wrong with you?" he said. "Come and look at the boy. He's got hurt playing with me and his mother's worried. What kind of a doctor are you?"

"He's fine," I said. "You can see it from here. Look at him rolling around. If he has that much movement in the knee there's no damage. All he wants is sympathy, which you're much better at giving."

"Don't be childish. At least put the mother's mind at rest."

Kate looked over at us at that moment. She had that hard stare of hers, the one that says, "I don't care, but make your mind up." It's the one she has when she stands behind her customers as they look in the mirror and try to tell her how they want their hair. Anyway, it made me go over.

"Hold still, Gareth. I can't help if you don't let me look at it." He stopped for a moment and looked at me and I lifted his leg and felt around the knee. "Does that hurt? That?" I looked thoughtful for a moment. I flexed his leg. "Well, Gareth, I would have to say that in my carefully considered opinion, what we've got here" — I paused for effect — "is a bad knee."

He didn't get it, but Kate did. She laughed out loud. She couldn't stop. She told me later it wasn't that funny. She was just so relieved. Gareth looked at her in amazement, but it made him forget his knee. She tried to say she was sorry, but when she saw his face she went off again.

"You better lay off football for a while," I said, and that's when my father promised he'd teach him how to fish and they marched down to the stream, leaving me alone with Kate.

PERSPECTIVE IN RENAISSANCE PAINTING

We sit at the back of the chapel. The coffin has been placed end on to the aisle rather than side on and from here it is hard to tell how long it really is. It looks about the size I'm used to. The discovery reminds me of perspective in Renaissance painting.

The coffin is closed, but the minister talks about Gareth's love of football and of Liverpool and I imagine him lying there in the red shirt he was always so proud of, with Ian Rush's number nine on the back.

Kate and her father are sitting in the front row. Her head is bowed, but her shoulders are still and I am sure she is dry-eyed. My father leans over and whispers in my ear, "I only wish we could have caught one fish. I promised him we'd get one." I shake my head. My father was supposed to take the boy fishing last week. He forgot when they were meeting and he was out shopping when Gareth came for him. The boy went to play in our drive while he waited. He was swinging on the stone gatepost when it toppled over on him. It was solid slate. It's still lying to one side of the drive, and I will offer to help carry it out of the way sometime. It will take two of us, although my father hurled it there by himself when he found the boy. Not that it made any difference.

There are only four pallbearers. The coffin rides on

their shoulders, but each with his free hand holds it in place as if it were so light it might just float away.

No one has said anything to us at the chapel, but when we get up to leave, two men slide into the pew on either side of us. I recognize the one next to me as the local grocer. He once told me that my father had bought a bar of soap off him every day for a week. Sure enough, under the sink at the cottage I found bar after bar after bar, but when I asked Father if he had some he said, "No, I think I must have run out."

"Sorry," the grocer says. "The family would prefer if you don't come to the grave."

Father hangs his head and looks at his hands.

"My father wants to pay his respects," I say. I'm watching people file out.

"The family would prefer if he stayed away."

"Did Kate say that?"

"The family."

The man next to my father says something to him in Welsh.

"What did he say? What did you say to my father? What did he say to you?"

No one answers.

"Take your father home," the grocer says.

"What did he say? I'm not going anywhere until I know what he said."

"He said, 'Are you satisfied?'"

"What the bloody hell does that mean?" I say. "It was an accident."

The grocer waits until the last person leaves and the four of us are alone in the chapel.

"A lot of people are saying it was negligence. They're saying it wouldn't have happened if your place had been properly kept up."

I get my father to his feet. The grocer puts his foot up on the pew in front to block the way. His leg is straight, and if he leaves it there I will stamp down and break it at the knee.

"Get out of my way. I'm taking him home." He lets us by.

"You do that," the grocer shouts after me. "Take him home. Take him back to England."

KATE HOPS FROM FOOT TO FOOT

Kate and I used to make love in the ugliest house. I would stand in the darkness beside the wall and when I heard the rattle of the chain holding the door shut I would step out. She brought blankets from her house and I brought a torch from my car. It was always too cold to undress. She would push my trousers down and I would lift her skirt. When I touched her breasts she would shy away and make me rub my hands together to warm them. She would hop from foot to foot while she waited for me to be warm enough to touch her.

Once I asked her if her father knew where she was going on the weekends when I was visiting. "I'm sure," she said. "But he knows better than to ask." I wondered, then, if she went out every weekend.

"Doesn't your father know?" she asked me back.

"I don't know," I said. "I don't think about it. He never brings it up."

"What would you do if he did?"

"I'd lie. I already lie. I tell him I come to see him."

"That's not a lie," she said. "Why else would you come?"

"I can't imagine."

"I'm serious."

"I come to see you."

"That's what you tell your father when you're lying. Why should I believe you?"

I lay on my back and looked up at the rough walls above me and thought of the people who built them. I wondered how they felt sleeping beneath them on that first night with all that precariously balanced weight around them. Did they have confidence in their balancing act? Maybe they drew lots.

Conversations with Kate were like a balancing act.

Another time she said to me, "If you're worried about your father being able to look after himself up here, you should take him away. I don't want to stop you doing what's right."

"You're not stopping me."

"I try to look in on him as often as I can."

"I appreciate that."

GRANDFATHER'S DOG

When we get home I tell my father I've decided to take him home with me the next morning. He says he's staying.

"Didn't you hear them? They think you're responsible. I'm not leaving you here."

"I am responsible. They're right. Who else's fault is it?"

"It doesn't have to be anybody's fault."

"I promised him. He was here because I promised him."

"You promised him you'd catch him a fish," I shout. "Don't be stupid. You're not responsible for his death. It was an accident. No one's responsible."

"This is my home," he says. "I can't leave."

"This is where you live. It's not your home. It hasn't been your home for forty years."

"Rubbish." He stands at the window and points. "My father lived over that hill and my uncle over that one. Did I ever tell you about them?"

"Yes," I say. "Lots of times."

It's a story about the time my grandfather's dog had a big litter and he told the family that they were not to sell any of the pups. His brother disobeyed him and told him the dogs had died. When my grandfather found out he'd sold them he never spoke to him again as long as he lived. My father says his uncle was the one who met him at the station when he came back from his national service in Germany to see Grandfather before he died. Even then the old man wouldn't see his brother. When I was a child I always thought it was a story about greed or about telling the truth, but that isn't it. It's not a story about my uncle. It's a story about my grandfather.

"Why weren't the puppies to be sold?" I say now.

"I can't remember," my father says. "It doesn't matter."

"Then what's the point of the story?"

"I don't know. Something about seeing things through."

"You're talking like a bloody idiot. You're as bad as these people. I'm not leaving here without you. You will be in that car tomorrow if I have to carry you."

THE DAM

In the late afternoon, my father gocs down the field to the stream. He's still in his black suit, with a spade on his shoulder, but I haven't the energy to fight with him. I'm sitting on our wall, watching Kate's house. I keep my eyes on the net curtains of her kitchen as I hear him splashing his way into the stream. The lights come on in her house; someone, not Kate or her father, comes out and pushes through the sheep who are clustered around the house for warmth. Whoever it is strides up the path and vanishes.

I hear him splashing and cursing behind me. If there is a fish in there still, it's too quick for him. I remember when we used to come on holiday up here and he would catch a dozen or more. He'd string grass stems through their gills and let me carry them in the door, although I never caught a single one. All he let me do at the river-bank was sit and touch the caught fish. I learned that they started out slick and became sticky as the afternoon wore on. Somewhere between the two states they died. He said that if I played with them and got used to the feel of them I'd learn how to catch them. He was wrong. It wasn't the feel of the fish I was afraid of. It was the feel of the unknown when I slid my fingers into the water. He probably couldn't have cured me, but he didn't try that hard — as long as I sat still and let him enjoy himself reliving his boyhood.

I see the door to the house open and shut again, and in the yellow light I see Kate. I assume she is making for the ugliest house and I pick up my torch and move to meet her, but then I see she is heading for my father and I quicken my pace.

"How are you?" I ask her gently.

"I just want to see your father," she says.

"Why?"

"I hear you had some trouble in the chapel and I wanted to say I'm sorry for it."

"They said it was his fault. You don't think that, do you?"

"It's all our faults," she says. "If you'd taken him home when you should have. If I hadn't given you a reason for letting him stay here."

"That's insane." She's talking like a relly. "It was an accident. A random accident. No one's to blame. No one's responsible. The gate was just loose."

I put my hand on her arm but she shrugs it off and strides on toward him. I follow, shaking my head.

She stands on the bank with her hands on her hips and looks down at him in the water. In the dusk the water is black except for where it bubbles white around his calves. She just looks at him for a long moment. I'm ready to put my hand over her mouth and carry her kicking and biting back to her father's house if necessary.

"Are there really fish in here still?" she says.

"I hope so," he says. "There always have been as long as I can remember."

"Show me how you catch them," she says, and he explains to her about trout tickling.

"Who taught you all that?"

"My father," he says. He turns and looks into the gloom. "Over there you could just see the road to our old house."

"You should come in," Kate says, and he smiles up at her tone and I almost think he is going to listen to her.

"Let me catch you a fish first." He winks at her.

"It's too dark, isn't it?"

"Not if you help me. This is my last chance. Will you?"

"What do you want me to do?"

"The surest way is to build a dam."

She takes the torch from me and holds it while he uses the spade to dig a narrow channel beside the stream. The stream is horseshoe-shaped at this point and he digs the trench from the start of the loop to the end of it. Lights are coming on in all the windows of the village on the hillside behind us.

"You're crazy," I say. "Both of you." But I take my own shoes and socks off and get down into the stream and begin moving rocks. I'm not having him manhandle them. The stream is so cold I lose the feeling in my feet in minutes. It makes it hard to keep my footing, but I work faster, thinking that even if I drop a rock on my toes I'll never feel it. I pile them up at the neck of the horseshoe and my father cuts the last yard of trench and water begins to rush down the channel. He lifts clumps of turf and throws them into the water to seal my dam and the water stops flowing into the horseshoe and begins to run out of it at the bottom. Kate stands at the other end beating the water, driving the fish back.

The level begins to drop slowly. The banks are revealed. Stones and gravel give way to mud.

"Shine the torch," my father says, and I take it from Kate and move it back and forth across the remaining water. It is brown from the mud at the bottom. We wait for any movement.

"There," Kate cries. She points, and in the light I see her arm is streaked with dirt. My father climbs down into the streambed, and mud flecks his trouser legs. He crouches over the shallow pool left in the centre of the stream and slides his hands in. He catches something and shouts, but loses his grip, and his hands thrash in the water. It is as if he is washing them. Finally he gets a grip and throws something up onto the bank. In the torchlight I see it is an eel, black and shiny. It twists in the grass and I take the spade and chop it in two. I turn around and with the torch I see my father on his knees in the streambed. He has his hands deep in the mud. Kate is standing over him with her hand on his shoulder. He is shaking.

"I know," she says. "Oh, I know."

"What are you doing?" I say. The torch plays back and forth from one face to the other. "What are you doing? It was an accident. It's nobody's fault. What are you doing?"

WHITEWASH

When I take him out to the car in the morning, we see that the walls have been covered in red graffiti. I don't speak Welsh, but even I know what Cymru am byth means. It's a nationalist slogan: "Wales forever."

I make my father sit in the car while I go and fetch the cans of whitewash from the shed. I wonder who did it. The grocer maybe. Maybe even Kate's father. I wonder if they were up here daubing it while we were down by the stream. It is nine o'clock on a Sunday morning and people are opening their curtains and fetching their newspapers. I imagine the whole hillside watching me as I paint over the slogan. Of course, I keep going. I've been wanting to do this for so long.

It takes me almost two hours to do the whole cottage and when I'm finished it shines in the bright morning light.

RELIEF

SOMETIME BETWEEN the cheese and the fruit, while the port was still being passed, Lieutenant Wilby allowed a sweet but rather too boisterous fart to slip between his buttocks. The company around the mess table was talking quietly, listening to the sound of the liquor filling the glasses, holding it up in the lamplight to relish its colour against the white canvas of the tent. It was, Lieutenant Bromhead had just explained, a bottle from General Chelmsford's own stock, and not the regulation port issued to officers. A hush of appreciation had fallen over the table.

Of course, Wilby had known the fart was coming, but it was much louder and more prolonged than he had anticipated, and the look of surprise on his face would have given him away even if Major Black, to his left, the port already extended, had not said, "Wilby!" in a sharp, shocked bellow.

"Sorry, sir," Wilby said. His face burned as if he'd been sitting in front of the hearth at home, reading by the firelight. He risked one quick glance up and around the table. "Sorry, sirs." Chaplain Pierce was looking down into his lap, exactly as he did when saying grace, and Captain Ferguson's moustache was jumping slightly at the corners, like the whiskers of a cat that had just scented a bowl of cream. Lieutenant Chard, however, sat just as he appeared in his photographs, his huge pale face tipped back like a great slab rising above his thick dark beard.

As for Bromhead, he looked only slightly puzzled. "What?" he said. "What is it?"

Wilby, staring down at the crumbs of Stilton on his plate, groaned inwardly. Bromhead's famed deafness was going to be the end of him.

He looked up under his brow as Bromhead's batman, who had just placed the fruit on the table, leaned forward and whispered all too audibly in his ear, "The lieutenant farted, sir."

"Chard?" Bromhead asked. Behind his beard, the older lieutenant turned the colour of claret. Bromhead himself wore only a thin moustache and sideburns, and Wilby thought he saw a flicker of a smile cross his face.

The batman leaned in to him again. "Wilby," he whispered.

"Ah," Bromhead said sadly. He stared at his glass. An uncomfortable silence fell over the mess table. Wilby's mortification was complete. And, perhaps because he wished himself dead, a small portion of his recent life flashed before his eyes.

The lieutenant had been suffering from terrible flatulence all the way from Helpmakaar. At first he had thought it was something to do with his last meal (a deer shot, several times, by Major Black, which he could hardly have refused in any case), but as the column approached Rourke's Drift, his bowels seemed in as great an uproar as ever. Fortunately, the ride had been made at a canter and he'd been able to clench his mount between his legs and smother the worst farts against his saddle — although the horse had tossed her head at some of the more drawn-out ones — but as they came in sight of the mission station, the major spurred them into a trot and then a gallop so that their pennant snapped overhead like a whip. Legs braced in the stirrups, knees bent, his body canted forward over his mount's neck, the lieutenant had had no choice but to release a crackling stream of utterance.

At first there was some undeniable relief in this, but as each dip and rise and tussock jarred loose further bursts, he was obliged to cry "Ya" and "Ho," as if encouraging his horse, to mask the worst outbreaks. He was grateful that over the drumming of hooves and the blare of the bugler who had hastily run out to welcome them to camp, no one seemed to notice, but the severity of the attack made him doubt that he had not soiled his breeches, and at the first opportunity he sought out the latrine to reassure himself.

Having put his mind at rest, seen to his tentage, and placed his horse in the care of the groom he shared with the other junior officers, Wilby had taken himself off to the perimeter of the camp. Despite the newly built walls and the freshly dug graves — they were overgrown already, but their silhouettes clearly visible in the long pale grass — it was all familiar to him from the articles in the *Army Gazette*, and in his mind he traced the events of the famous defence that had been fought there not three months before.

Fewer than a hundred able-bodied men, a single company plus those left behind at the mission hospital, had fought off a force of some five thousand Zulus — part of the same *impi* that had wiped out fifteen hundred men at Isandhlwana the previous day. They had held out for upwards of ten hours of continuous close fighting and inflicted almost five hundred casualties on the enemy. It was a glorious tale, and Wilby didn't need to look at the page from the *Gazette* that he kept in his tunic pocket to recall all the details. He had read and reread it so often on the ride out from Durban that it felt as fragile as an illuminated manuscript. "You'd think it was a love letter," the major had scoffed.

He should be rejoicing to be here, standing on the ground of the most famous battle in the world, and yet he felt only the churning of his wretched stomach. Tomorrow they would ride out, the first patrol to visit the site of Isandhlwana since the massacre.

He stared off in the direction they would take in the morning. The ferry across the drift was moored about two hundred yards away, and on the far bank the track ran beside the river for a half-mile or so and then cut away over a low rise and out of sight. Wilby found himself thinking of the Derbyshire countryside near his home . . . and fishing — up to his thighs in the dark cool water, feeling the pull of the current but dry inside his thick leather waders. He supposed the sight of the river must have brought it to mind.

It was Ferguson who found him out there. He saw the captain running toward him, his red tunic among the waving grass, shouting his news.

"Wils, we are invited to dine with Bromhead and Chard. You, myself, the major, and Pierce."

"Truly?" Wilby caught his friend's arm, and Ferguson stooped for a moment to catch his breath. Then he shook himself free and took a step back, squared his shoulders and held up his hand as if reading from a card.

"Lieutenants Bromhead and Chard request the pleasure of Major Black and his staff's company for dinner in their mess at eight o'clock."

Of course, it was a little unusual for two lieutenants to invite a major to dinner, but by then Bromhead and Chard were expected to be made majors themselves — not to mention the Victoria Crosses everyone was predicting — and the breach of etiquette seemed altogether forgivable to Wilby. A dinner with Gonville Bromhead and Merriot Chard was simply the most sought-after invitation in the whole of Natal in the spring of 1889.

"Good Lord, Fergie," he said. "Why, I must change."

He had spent the next hour in his suspenders and undershirt, polishing the buttons of his tunic, slipping a small brass plate behind them to protect the fabric and then working the polish into the raised regimental crests and burnishing them to a glow. Next he worked on his boots, smearing long streaks of bootblack up and down, working them into the hide with a swift circular motion and then bringing the leather to a shine with a stiff brush. He thought hard about the thin beard and moustache he had begun to grow three weeks before and with a sigh pulled out his razor. Ferguson, waxing his own moustache, paused and watched him in silence, but Wilby refused to meet his eye. His moustache would never be as good as the captain's anyway. Fergie's handlebar was justly famous in the regiment, said to be wide enough for troopers riding behind him to see both ends. Wilby knew that wasn't quite true. The captain had made him check, with Wilby standing behind him trying to make out both waxed tips. In the end they had had to call in the chaplain, and standing shoulder to shoulder, about five feet behind Ferguson, Wilby and Pierce had each been able to see a tip of moustache on either side.

Wilby lathered the soap in his shaving mug and applied it with the badger-hair brush his father had given him before he'd come out on campaign. The razor was dull and he had to pause to strop it, but he managed to shave without drawing blood.

Finally, he extracted his second set of epaulettes and his best collar from the tissue paper he kept them in and had Ferguson fix them in place. The fragrant smell of hair oil filled their tent as they each in turn vigorously applied a brush to the other's tunic. Without a decent mirror, they paused and scrutinized each other carefully, then bowed deeply — Wilby from the waist,

Ferguson taking a step back and dropping his arm in a flourish.

The meal had gone well at first. The major had introduced him to first Chard and then Bromhead and he'd looked them both in the eyes (Chard's gray, Bromhead's brown) and shaken hands firmly. In between, he had made to clasp his hands behind his back and been sure to rub them on his tunic to ensure they were dry. "How do you do, sir?" he had said to each in turn.

"Very well," Chard had said in his gruff way.

"Splendid," Bromhead had told him a little too loudly. The story of Bromhead's deafness — that he would almost certainly have been pensioned off if his older brother had not been on Chelmsford's staff — was well known among the junior officers. It was said that he had only been given B company of the 2nd/24th because it was composed almost entirely of Welshmen and it was thought that his deafness wouldn't be so noticeable or important to men who spoke English with such an impenetrable accent. There was even a joke that Bromhead's company had only received its posting at Rourke's Drift because the lieutenant thought the general had been offering him more *pork rib* at the mess table. "Rather," he was reputed to have said. "Very tasty."

Some of the officers still made fun of Bromhead, but Wilby put it down to simple jealousy. For his own part, he thought it more, not less, heroic that Bromhead had overcome his disability. He had a theory that amid all the noise of battle a deaf man might have an advantage, might come to win the respect of men hoarse from shouting and deafened by the report of their arms.

At dinner, Wilby had waited until the major and Ferguson had each made some remark or other, nodded at each response, and echoed the chaplain's compliments on the food. Only then, as the batman passed the gravy boat among them, did he ask a question of his own.

"How does it feel?" he said. "I mean, how does it feel to be heroes?"

Bromhead looked at him closely for a moment, but it was Chard who answered.

"Well," he began. He stroked his beard, and it made an audible rasping sound. "I would have to say, principally, the sensation is one of relief. Relief to be alive after all — not like the poor devils you'll see tomorrow — but also relief to have learned some truth about myself. To have found I am possessed of — for want of a better word — courage."

"I say," murmured Ferguson. He grinned at Wilby.

What a blowhard, Bromhead thought. It pained him that Chard's name and his own should be so inextricably linked. Bromhead and Chard. Chard and Bromhead. He felt like a blasted vaudevillian.

"It's an ambition fulfilled," Chard went on, ignoring the interruption. "Since I was a little chap I remember wondering — as who has not? — if I were a brave fellow. Cowardice, funk — more than any imagined beast or goblin, that was my great terror. And now I have my answer." He paused and looked around the table slowly, and this time it was harder for Wilby to hold his gaze. "If the chaplain will be so good as to forgive me, I rather fancy it is as if I have stood before Saint Peter himself, not knowing if I were a bally sinner or no, and dashed me if he hasn't found my name there among the elect."

The chaplain smiled and bobbed his head complacently. Wilby and Ferguson glanced at each other again, their eyes bright but not quite meeting in their excitement.

"Heavens!" said Bromhead, clearing his throat. "For my part, being a hero is nothing so like how I fancy a beautiful young debutante must feel." There was a puzzled round of laughter, but Wilby saw Chard press his lips together — a white line behind his dark beard — and kept his own features still. "You've seen them at balls, gentlemen, there are one or two each season, those girls who aren't quite sure but then discover all of a sudden quite how delightful they are. Oh, I don't know. Perhaps their mamas had told them so, but they'd not believed them. After all, that's what mamas are for. They'd not known whether to listen to their doting fathers and all those old loyal servants, surely too ugly to know what was beautiful or not anymore. And then, in one evening, confound it, they know. And all around them, suddenly, why who but our own good selves, gentlemen — suitors all."

Wilby could see Ferguson smile, and he knew he was thinking of Ethel, his betrothed. He had seen such women as Bromhead described, but his own smile was more rueful. (He remembered one long conversation with a certain Miss Fanshaw, who had cheerfully told him that she had sent no less than five white feathers to men she knew at the time of the Crimea — "And you know," she had told him earnestly, "not one of them returned home alive.") The major he knew would be thinking of his wife, home in Bath, and the chaplain, he supposed, of God. He saw Chard, bored, study his reflection in the silverware.

"Anyway," the major said. "Put us out of our misery. Let's hear the details of this famous defence of yours, eh? Give us the story from the horse's mouth, so to speak."

"Oh, well." Bromhead opened his hands. "It was fairly fierce, I suppose. The outcome was in doubt for some hours." He faltered, and Wilby, who had been leaning forward eagerly, sat back and saw the others look disappointed. This was, after all, what they had come for.

Chard, however, stepped in. He was an officer of engineers and he believed in telling a tale correctly.

He told them about the hours of hand-to-hand combat, of the bayonets that the men called lungers, and of the assegais of the Zulus. How the men's guns had become so hot from firing that they cooked off rounds as soon as they were loaded, causing the men to miss; so hot that the soft brass shell casings melted in the breeches and had to be dug out with a knife before the whole futile process could begin again. He told them about men climbing up on the wall they'd built of biscuit boxes and mealie bags and lunging down into the darkness; of the black hands reaching up to grab the barrels and the shrieks of pain when they touched the hot glowing metal — shrieks that were oddly louder than the soft grunts men gave as a bayonet or assegai found its mark. He told them about the sound of bullets clattering into the biscuit boxes at the base of the wall and rustling in the mealie bags nearer the top, so that you knew the Zulus were getting their range. He described men overpowered, dragged from the walls, surrounded by warriors. How the Zulus knocked them down and ripped open their tunics, and the popping sound of buttons flying loose. "That would be the last sound a lot of our chaps heard," he said. With their tunics open, the Zulus would disembowel them, opening men from balls to breastbone with one swift strike.

"I swear I'll never be able to see another button pop loose from a shirt without thinking of it," Chard said. He took a sip of wine. "Of course, you'll see a good deal of that handiwork tomorrow, I'll warrant."

That was when Wilby began to feel his flatulence return, and his discomfort grew even when Bromhead broke in and explained that the Zulus believed that opening a man's chest was the only way to set his spirit free from his dead body.

"Really, it's an act of mercy as they see it," he said. "I hope so, at least. There was one poor chap of mine, a Private Williams. Bit of a no-account, but a decent sort. I saw him get fairly dragged over the wall before I caught hold his leg. This was quite in the thick of it. There were so many Zulus trying to rush us from all sides, they were like water swirling round a rock in a stream. Quite a ghastly tug of war I had for him with them. Every time they had him to their side he'd give one of those little grunts Chard was talking about, but then I'd pull like mad, and when I had him more to me he'd look up and say in a cheery way, 'Much obliged, sir.'

In the end, they began to swarm over the walls all about us and I had to let him go to draw my pistol. I told him I was sorry — I fancied he'd be in a bad panic, you know — but he just said, 'Not at all, sir,' and 'Thank you kindly, sir.'"

Bromhead paused.

"I was going to write to his people. Say how sorry I was I couldn't save him. But dashed if he didn't join up under a false name. A lot of the Welshmen do, it seems. For a long time I thought they were all just called Evans and Williams and Jones and what-have-you, but it turns out that those are just the most obvious false names for them to choose. His blamed leg — you know, I can't get it out of my mind, how remarkably warm it was."

He sat back, and the batman took the opportunity to step forward with the port. Bromhead watched in silence as the glasses filled with redness.

Wilby had managed a few quiet expulsions, but then came the surprising and ruinous fart.

The silence around the table seemed to go on for hours — Wilby could hear the pickets calling out their challenge to the final patrols of the evening. Finally Bromhead looked over and said genially, "Preserved potatoes." He shook his head. "Make you fart like a confounded horse."

He waved his man forward with the cigars, and as they passed around he leaned in toward the table and looked around at them all.

"Reminds me of a story," he said, cutting the end of his cigar. "I haven't thought of it in years, mind you —

about a bally Latin class, of all things." He ran the end of the cigar around his tongue and raised his chin for the batman to light him. "Hardly the story you expected to hear, but I'll beg your indulgence." He took a mighty puff and began.

"Well, we had this old tyrant of a master — Marlow, his name was — of the habit of making us work at our books in silence every other afternoon. Any noise and he would beat you with a steel ruler that he carried from his days in the navy. Now that was fear. I swear it was rumoured among us — a rumour spread no doubt by older lads to put a fright on us — that boys had lost fingers, chopped clean off at the knuckle by that ruler.

"I must have been upwards of twelve or so. I can't recall quite the circumstances, but I'd bent over from my desk to retrieve a pen I'd dropped — or more likely some blighter had thrown — on the floor. We were always trying to get some other poor bugger to make a sound and bring down the tyrant's wrath upon his head, but anyhow, as I say, I'd bent over to pick up my pen — I was in the middle of translating 'Horatio on the Bridge' or some such rot — and what do you know but I farted. Quite surprised myself. Quite taken aback, I was. Not that it was an especially, you know, loud one. More of a pop really. Or a squeak. Hang me if that's not it either. Let's just say somewhere between a pop and a squeak. Hardly a decent fart at all — if the truth be told, it's rather astonishing I can remember it so well. No matter. Whatever the precise sound of the expulsion, in that room with everyone trying to be still it was like a bally pistol shot, like the crack of a whip.

"Well, the fellows behind me, of course, went off into absolute fits and gales. Up jumps the tyrant, brandishing his ruler, and I fancy I'm for the high jump now. The whole room falls silent as the grave as the old man stalks up the aisle between our desks, looking hard all about him.

"'John Beddows,' he says to one of the chaps behind me, and his voice is veritable steel, 'would you mind telling me what is the source of this hilarity?'

"'Nothing, sir,' says John — a decent enough sort, loafer that he was — and I begin to think I might be spared, but dash me if the old man doesn't persist.

"'Nothing,' he says. 'You had to be laughing at something, boy. Only idiots laugh at nothing. Are you an idiot, Mister Beddows?' And he bent that ruler in his hands.

"'No, sir,' says John, pulling a long face. 'Please, sir. Gonville Bromhead farted, sir.'"

Wilby glanced around the table and saw that Ferguson was grinning broadly, his teeth showing around his cigar. The chaplain, too, was struggling to keep a straight face, and even Major Black had a curious look in his eye. Only Chard showed no glimmer of humor. He had stubbed out his cigar and taken an apple, which he was chewing steadily.

"Of course," Bromhead went on, "you can imagine the pandemonium. You'd have thought there was a murder in progress, and to be honest I could have cheerfully strangled Beddows. I let out a swear or two under my breath, but the tyrant himself was at a loss for a moment. All I could do was snatch my hands up from where they'd been lying on the desk and press them into my pockets.

"'Silence!' the tyrant finally bellowed, and then, with me cringing, 'That's quite enough drollery, gentlemen. Back to work. All of you.'

"Of course, it was only a reprieve of sorts. The worst was still to come. By and by we came out for our break and the other chaps started up a game of tag. I was too angry or ashamed to join them. I took myself off to a corner of the yard and watched. One person would be on, his tie would be undone, and he'd tag another, who'd also pull his tie open, and they'd keep tagging until they all had their ties hanging loose. Only when some of them ran closer to me did I catch the name of the game. 'Funky Farters.'" Bromhead looked around him, his face a mask of tragedy.

"That dashed game became the craze at school for months, although I can tell you I never played it. I had dreams, nightmares really, of boys going home at the holidays and teaching it to their friends and in this way the detestable game — and my disgrace — spreading to every darned school in England. Can you imagine? I couldn't shake the notion. I thought with certitude that affair would be the only thing I'd be known for in my whole life. I thought, *I'll die and my only lasting contribution to this life will be a fart in a confounded Latin class.*"

The table was roaring with laughter by now, the chaplain dabbing at his eyes with his napkin, Ferguson clutching his sides, and the major positively braying. Ash from the almost extinguished cigar in his hand peppered the table as he shook. Wilby found himself laughing too, uncontrollably relieved. He caught Bromhead's eye and the older lieutenant nodded.

The meal broke up shortly after — the major's patrol would have to leave camp at first light — and the men went out into the night to find their own tents. Bromhead leaned back in his chair and watched the major sidle up to Wilby and Ferguson and say, "I remember once letting loose a mighty one on parade in India," and the two young officers staggered with laughter. The chaplain was the last to leave. He smiled at Bromhead and shook his head. "An edifying tale." Then he hurried after the other three, and Bromhead saw him put an arm around Wilby's shoulder.

Only Chard stalked off alone, his back straight and his chin held high. "Now that man," Bromhead said to his batman, "mark my words, has never farted in his life. It'd break his back to let rip now." He lit another cigar and smoked it thoughtfully while the batman cleared the plates from the table.

"It's a terrible thing being afraid, Watkins, do you not think?"

The batman said he thought it was.

"Join me," Bromhead said, and he poured out two glasses of the celebrated port and they sat and drank in silence for a moment.

"Bloody rum thing. Zulus thinking to find a fellow's soul in his entrails, eh?"

The batman nodded. The port tasted like syrup to him, and later he would need a swig of his squareface —

the army-issue gin in its square bottle — to take the taste away.

It was late, and the light breeze through the tent felt cold to Bromhead. He always took more of a chill when he'd been drinking. He pulled a blanket off the cot behind him and draped it around his shoulders. "Like an old woman," he said. He wrapped his arms around himself under the blanket, clutching his shoulders, and thought again how really remarkably *warm* Private Williams's leg had felt.

"Wake me," he said to the batman, "before the major's patrol leaves in the morning. I think I should like to see them off."

A UNION

MAY 1899

On the first day of the strike, Thomas Jones pulled on his white flannel shirt and shook out his breeches. A thin gray dust rose into the bedroom. He held the trousers up and slapped the double-lined seat vigorously.

"How many times do I have to tell you? Do that outside," his wife, Catrin, called up from the kitchen. Her voice carried clearly through the thin floor, and Thomas could tell she was standing at the sink.

"What?" He shook the trousers once more to disperse the dust and pulled them on quickly. "What's that you say?"

"I can *hear* you," she said. "And I'm not such a fool that I can't see slate dust on my bedspread every morning."

Thomas wrapped a thin leather belt around his waist and fixed his best chisel in it.

"You could always shake them out the window," she called.

"And give the neighbors a nasty turn?" he said, coming down the stairs and pulling a face for the boys.

"You'd be hearing about it in chapel quicker than you can say —"

"Knife!" Dafydd shouted.

"Old baldy Price would love that for a sermon."

Arthur was laughing so much he was coughing up milk and Catrin had to take his glass and slap him on the back.

"Hush, will you? You shouldn't teach them to laugh at the reverend. Here," she said, taking the boys' plates, "make some room for your father."

Dafydd went off to get ready for school. Arthur sat down on the rug near the fire where he had left his toy tools the night before. It was the middle of May and they hadn't had a fire in the grate since April, but habit kept him playing in the same place. He took his wooden mallet and chisel and started to tap at the slate fireplace.

Catrin buttered the cut end of the loaf and carved Thomas a thick white slice while he poured sugar into his cup of tea.

"So you're all dressed up with nowhere to go," she said.

"Nothing's decided yet. We're just having a meeting."

"On company time?"

He shrugged and took a bite of bread.

"You're asking for trouble."

"I've never known management to give us what we asked for yet."

She leaned back against the sink and watched him chew slowly.

"You're like a cow with its cud."

With his mouth still full, he toasted her with his teacup.

"I hope you haven't forgotten what today is?" she said.

"What's that, then? Christmas?"

"The twelfth. The clock comes today." She meant the grandfather clock they had been saving for all year. The crowning touch to her parlour.

"How could I forget? It's costing me an arm and a leg."

She crossed her arms and looked at him.

"And that'll still be all right, will it?"

"Listen," he said quickly, realizing the mistake. "That's your clock. I promised it you and it's worth every penny. What's a man's house, if he can't tell the time in it?"

She studied him for a moment and he met her gaze steadily. Then he folded the last of his bread and butter, pushed it whole into his mouth, and winked at her.

"*Mochin!*" she said.

Grinning, he got to his feet and fetched his black bowler hat from the shelf by the door. He set it straight on his head and reached for his umbrella in the corner.

"What do you want that for? It's going to be another scorcher."

"Oh, you know." He hefted it in his hand. "Just a feeling." He swished the umbrella back and forth quickly through the air.

"Wait for me," Dafydd called. He had his books strapped up in an old belt, dangling from his hand.

"You make your own way to school this morning," his father said quickly.

"Why can't I walk with you?"

Thomas went over to the boy and held the bowler over his head for a second. "Still too big," he said. "I expect I must be in charge here a bit longer. Help your mother with the dishes before you go."

"But I'll be late."

"Worried about being late for school!" his father cried. "It must be a red-letter day, Mother."

"Must be," she said quietly.

He put his hat back on, pointed at each of them once with the steel tip of his umbrella, and went out the door. They heard the tap of the metal twice on the slate of the garden path and then he was gone.

At the end of his row of terrace houses, Thomas paused for a moment. High Street before him was filled with grim-faced quarrymen. Bowler hats bobbed along on a sea of white, and he waited until he heard his name and saw a hand raised.

It was 123 Davies, although Thomas didn't need the raised hand to see that. 123 stood a head taller than the rest of the crowd and if that wasn't enough, his bowler, the largest stocked by Nelson's in Caernarfon, was still a size too small for him and always had to be kept in place with one hand. With both arms held above his head, 123 looked like he was wading through the crowd.

"Shouldn't you be up the front?" Thomas asked him. He had to shout to be heard over the sound of boots in the street. "I'd have thought they could use fellows like you on a day like this."

"Told me to hang back, if you can believe it," the big man bellowed, making a space in the stream of bodies for Thomas to join him.

123 Davies was a bad-rock man, and a slate dresser like Thomas Jones wouldn't normally have been seen with him except that he was Catrin's older brother. As a lad, Thomas had worked beside 123's father, learning how to see the slate, how to look at a slab and know where the faults lay and how the rock would cleave and split. It was said that old Davies's slates came off his chisel *fel menyn* — like butter — but 123 was so lacking in skill it was almost a scandal. At sixteen he had been the oldest *rubbler*, or apprentice, the mine had ever had. His father refused to walk to work with him and his mother despaired of his ever earning enough to marry and give her grandchildren. Thomas himself had become a journeyman at fourteen, at about the time that 123 had taken the king's shilling and joined the Welsh Guards. He spent ten years as an infantryman in Africa and only came home when his father died. That was when he had taken up as a bad-rock man, building the huge mounds of waste slate behind the quarry, to keep his mother.

In the pub his first night back, Davies had brandished a Zulu spear he had brought home with him and drunk them all under the table. Somewhere in that evening he had explained that there were so many Davieses and Joneses in the Guards that the English officers had taken to calling them by their enlisted numbers. Of course, after that night no one could actually remember what his number had been, so un-dau-tri, 123, was what stuck. Catrin and her mother were the only ones who still called him Roy. Thomas always used his nickname, and even the boys called him Uncle 123, despite their mother's protests.

By the time they'd climbed the hill behind the village and reached the gates of the quarry, there must have been at least six hundred men squeezed onto the path before them. More men, those who were coming from villages in the valley, began to spread out onto the farmland to either side. Over their heads, Thomas could see the upper terraces of the quarry rising up the hillside, curving gently toward him. He named them to himself: Victoria, Disraeli, Livingston, Nightingale. Their faceted faces gleamed dully around the dark mouths of sinkholes and the galleries gaping behind them. He saw that the panniers on the Blondin — the cableway, named after the famous tightrope walker — were motionless, but he followed the thin slant line of the steel hawser as it rose up to the topmost terraces, Ceiling and Garret.

There was some commotion at the front of the crowd he couldn't make out, but 123, who had a clear view, told him the rubblers were just chasing sheep for a game.

"What about at the gate?" Thomas asked.

"There's four constables, Mr. Randall, and Dewi Parry." These latter were the manager and foreman of the quarry.

"Doing what?" Thomas said.

"Nothing much. Standing around. Randall's smoking his pipe. Parry keeps going behind the office." He laughed. Behind the office was the privy.

"Too much tea," Thomas said. "He drinks as much as the rest of us, but he's not got enough dust in his lungs to soak up a thimbleful. Who's at the front for us?"

"Ellis Roberts and Merfyn Hughes," 123 said, catching sight of the chairman and secretary of the union. Ellis was an experienced quarryman, well respected for his skill at blasting the huge slabs of slate from the work face; Hughes had lost a hand in a quarry accident as a boy and become the local schoolmaster, known to Dafydd and the other lads as "Merv the Swerve" for his erratic riding of his prized bicycle.

"There's the Reverend Price, too," 123 said, and Thomas rolled his eyes.

"Don't look straight at him in this sun," he said, running his hand over his head to smooth his hair down. "The shine could blind you."

Ellis Roberts spoke first. The story was the one Thomas had heard yesterday in the quarry. How Bobby Griffiths, one of the younger men, had been called out the night before to see his mother in the valley. The old woman was ill and not expected to live, and sure enough, she had died in the night. Griffiths had come back up the hill to work the next morning, notwithstanding, but, arriving twenty minutes late, had been docked a day's pay on account of not getting written permission for his absence. When a deputation was sent to plead the boy's case, they were all suspended a week for leaving the work face.

An ugly murmur ran through the crowd, and here and there angry cries of "Shame!" rang out.

"They say their rules are good enough for factories in Liverpool and Manchester," Roberts said when the noise had died down. "Good enough for the English, maybe. But not for Welshmen. Not for quarrymen. Not for any *men* at all. Mr. Randall says it's only a formality, and that may be, but what do we need with formalities in a quarry? There's no 'by your leave' around a blasting cap. I say where permission is asked, it can be given *or* refused."

Thomas felt a push at his back and leaned into it.

"Are we children," Roberts called, "that we should hold up our hands and ask, 'Please, sir'? Are we beasts that we should be herded by the dogs of Capital? We are men, I tell you. And all we ask is to be treated as such."

The pressure behind Thomas was growing. The chin of the man behind him butted his shoulder and he heard teeth snap. Someone nearby shouted, "Stop shoving," and from behind him a voice snarled back, "Says who?" The crowd heaved forward, pressing him against the back of the man in front, and Thomas gripped his umbrella harder.

"What's going on at the front?" he called to 123.

"People are getting pushed up against the gates. The constables have got their truncheons out, but the lads are jabbing 'em through the bars with their brollies."

The crowd surged again and Thomas had to fight to keep his footing. When he looked up 123 was yards away from him. He heard shrill police whistles, and turning toward the quarry, he saw the tops of the gates jerking back and forth and he knew the men were pulling on them. As he watched, he saw the gates rise up and he thought, *They're lifting them off their hinges*. Ellis Roberts appeared, shinning up the ironwork. The crowd roared, thinking he was going over, but halfway up he twisted an arm through the bars and turned to face them.

"Quiet!" someone yelled, and the cry was taken up until the crowd settled enough for them to hear the union leader.

"He's calling for silence," the man next to him said, but Thomas called, "No, he wants a *minute's* silence. For Mrs. Griffiths. Out of respect."

He arched his back against the man behind him until the pressure lessened. Then he bowed his head along with the rest of the crowd.

The pause took the steam out of the men. Roberts called on the Reverend Price to speak next. He came to protest the loss of the Ascension Day holiday, which the men had used to take the Thursday after Easter. That spring it had been denied by the quarry managers, who claimed it was an unofficial holiday. What that meant, according to the reverend, was that it was not an Anglican holiday. The reverend was a third-generation Nonconformist preacher, himself. "The very day that Christ should rise up to His Father's right hand has been struck from the calendar. His last day on this earth, His last hours in the society of men. Now, I am no politician, but it seems to me that in the ledger you're owed that holiday. No matter what else the company may say."

There would be services appropriate to the day, the reverend told them, his bald head nodding up and down, but by then the men were beginning to melt away from the edge of the crowd, the *rubblers* first, carrying the news down the hill and through the village. Before long the streets were filled with running men, holding their hats on their heads, with children coming out of classes and shopgirls leaving their counters, none of them wanting to miss one more minute of the holiday.

"So?" Catrin said, when he stepped into the kitchen.

"No strike today," he said, propping his umbrella in the corner. "Just a holiday."

"And tomorrow?"

"Will take care of itself, no doubt."

The latch on the kitchen door clattered again and Dafydd burst in, breathless and red-faced. He stopped guiltily and looked at his parents.

"Holiday indeed," Catrin said. "Now I've three of you underfoot instead of one."

"That's easily fixed. I'll take this one down the beach," Thomas told her. To Dafydd he added, "Bring the bike round and fetch your football."

"Do you think the carter will come with the clock if it's a holiday?"

"Don't be daft. The rev can say what he likes about

Christ hanging round Bethany since Ascension Day, but he can't declare a holiday for the whole county. Besides, for twelve guineas, Carter would be here on Judgment Day."

"Perhaps you should stay," she said. "You could be here to pay him yourself."

"Don't tell me you need help to spend money now."

"It's a lot of money."

"Make up your mind," he said. "You want me here, or you want me out from under your feet?" He looked hard at her for a moment. "Right. I'll take the boy now and I'll be back early. If I know Carter, he'll do his business in town and head up here last thing. That way he can have a few drinks without his missus knowing anything."

He could hear the boy bouncing the ball on the slate step outside and he gave her a brief kiss and whispered, "Cheer up. It's a holiday." She followed him to the door and watched him swing the boy onto the handlebars. He put the ball in his son's hands and, with one foot on a peddle, pushed the bike off. It wobbled a moment, picking up speed. Then he swung his other leg over the back wheel and settled himself in the saddle. Without looking back, he raised one hand to wave.

It usually took twenty minutes by bike to the beach at Dinas Dinlle, but today, with the crowds of men and boys on the road, it took almost forty. The brakes on the bike squeaked all the way. Halfway down, Thomas found the bowler on his head too hot in the sun and slipped it over his son's ears. From there it soon found its way onto the football, where Dafydd held it in place with his thumbs. Finally, on the stony Dinas beach, Thomas put a handful of smooth pebbles inside it to stop it rolling away in the breeze and sat down beside it.

Dafydd went off with the other lads and Thomas watched 123 Davies join them. Soon the big man was refereeing a game in the distance, the ball flying up erratically off the stones and the boys charging after it in their boots. By the water, a group of smaller children had two umbrellas open and upended in the shallows. They bobbed slowly down the shore. A couple of the men stood nearby in case one of the kids should fall, but otherwise they were all sitting or lying on the beach, in small groups or alone. Some had their shoes and socks off and were rolling up their breeches. A couple of the older men had knotted the corners of their handkerchiefs to put over their heads against the bright sun. Thomas found himself sitting cross-legged with a smooth stone in his hand. He hadn't even been aware of picking it up until he started bouncing it in his palm. It had a pleasing weight, and even when it slipped through his fingers and clacked against the other stones before him it made a soothing sound. He collected a handful of smaller stones and poured them from hand to hand, listening to the noise they made.

After a time he got to his feet and walked down to the shore. He tossed a stone a few more times in his hands and bent and flipped it, underarm, over the water. It skipped three times and then vanished with a small pop.

He stooped and picked up another stone and sent that one skimming over the waves as well. Four skips. He began to walk along the water's edge with his head down, looking for smooth flat pebbles. Every time he found a good one he flipped it out across the water. Some promising ones he slipped in his trouser pockets.

123 fell into step beside him with a nod. When Thomas stopped next, the other man bent and skipped a stone six times, almost thirty yards out over the water. Thomas sent one after it, almost as far, but only five skips. Pretty soon they were sending stones one after another, and two or three other men walked down the sloping beach to join them. Some stood, barefoot, in the shallows, some on land. The group of them drifted slowly along the beach as they ran out of good stones in one place. Dafydd and the other boys came back and helped to collect more.

Once, one of the littler lads brought over a handful of shells instead of stones. 123 bent down to him with a smile. "What are these good for, then?" he said, and the child pressed one to his ear with a grin. He held out another to the big man, who laughed.

Thomas tired of the game soon enough, but sat close by to watch the others. 123 came over and squatted beside him.

"What's your best?"

"Twelve, I think. It gets hard to count at the end."

"Nine for me."

They were silent for a moment and Thomas could hear the clack of stones as the big man shifted his weight.

"How long do you think the strike'll last, then?" he said at length.

Thomas watched a miner bend his hips and send a stone skipping over the water.

"After this morning's performance?" he asked. The big man shrugged. "About as long as it does."

"I mean, you know Mair Morris and I are engaged, in a manner of speaking."

"You either are or you aren't, I'd say."

"Well, I've been saving up for us," his brother-in-law said. "I started off putting a bit by to take Mother to Rhyl for a holiday, but now she says she wants grandchildren, not a holiday. Not that she doesn't love your lads," he added quickly. "She just wants *Tad's* name to go on." He paused. "So how long do you think the strike fund will last?"

"'Bout as long as the strike. You know, if I were a bachelor, I shouldn't be in too much of a hurry to marry. You think it's hard work up on that rock pile."

"Ah, there's no romance in you old married blokes. What's a man without a wife, anyway? Hardly a man at all, as you might say. You've been spoiled is what. Having a good trade and being able to marry as young as you did. You never had to wait for nothing."

"Ha!"

"Well," 123 said at last, "I suppose it does no good worrying."

Thomas nodded slowly and stared out at the waves.

"Slates from here get shipped all over," he said. "Germany, America, India. What's the world going to do for a roof over its head without us?" He paused and looked across at the big man. "Mair Morris, eh?" He knew her slightly, her father, Cyril, being one of the oldest slate dressers in the quarry. "What's a lovely girl like that see in you?" The big man grinned. "Be all over by Christmas, you'll see. You can wait for it that long."

He took the chisel from his belt and dug it into the loose stones before him. Finding a promising one, he rested it on his thigh, placed the chisel against it, and began to tap it with another large stone for a mallet. 123 looked at his long fine fingers curled around the chisel and the stone.

"You'll never split that," he said. "That's granite, that is."

"I'm not trying," Thomas told him. "I just want the sound of it."

Before them, at the water's edge, a few of the men stopped their throwing and turned to look. Their arms cocked again and the stones skipped off the water.

It was past five o'clock when Thomas and Dafydd left the beach and it took almost an hour to push the bike all the way uphill to Bethany. Dafydd sat on the saddle and his father pushed. When they arrived it was close to Thomas's normal homecoming time and he felt almost as tired after the long climb from the coast as from a day at the quarry. He was thinking so hard about what to tell Catrin that he only realized in the fields below the town that his pockets were still filled with small stones from the beach and he emptied them at the side of the lane.

The cart was waiting in the street outside the house when they arrived. Thomas leaned the bike up against the wall and lifted Dafydd up to look. There was a coarse cloth made of half a dozen sacks sewn together, and when he turned it down they saw the grandfather clock, on its back, staring up at the sky. At first all Thomas saw was the reflection of clouds in the varnish and he had to shift his position to look at it properly. He pointed out for Dafydd the revolving panel set in the face, with the sun and moon painted in gold and silver, and the intricate carved scrollwork at the crown tapering away to a slender pinnacle. He ran his hand up it and let his finger rest for a moment on the point.

He whistled softly.

"There's lovely, eh?"

When they went inside, he found Carter sitting at the table drinking tea with Catrin.

"There he is," the man cried. "I was just telling your missus, Mr. Jones, that I'd have to be getting home soon."

Thomas nodded to his wife.

"Calm yourself, man. It's only just opening time now."

"I was beginning to think you'd had second thoughts."

"Why's that?"

"On account of the strike."

Thomas looked at him steadily.

"What strike is that, then? All this is is a holiday."

"I didn't mean anything by it," the carter said, getting to his feet. "You know your own business, of course, I'm sure."

"Right enough. Let's have a look at her, shall we?"

He watched the carter knock back his tea and move toward the door. Thomas was about to follow him when Catrin touched his arm.

"I'll just have a look at it and tell him I don't want it," she whispered. "Say I've changed my mind."

He couldn't look at her then. He just squeezed her hand.

"It's yours if you want it," he said gruffly, and he was glad when the carter shouted from the door, "Mr. Jones. Today, if you please."

"Righto."

They carried it like a long body between them from the cart to the gate, white-faced with the effort but saying nothing of it to each other. In the gateway, Thomas got down on his haunches and the carter began to tilt the clock to a standing position. Thomas pressed his cheek to the front panel and took the weight onto his fingertips. The wood felt slippery against his face, damp with sweat, and he could feel his fingers beginning to slide against the veneer. He shifted quickly to get a better grip and the clock lurched. The lock on the pendulum inside came unclasped and the street was suddenly filled with chimes. With his ear against the clock, it felt to Thomas as if the chimes were striking inside him, but he held steady, his heart racing at the thought of dropping the precious thing. He was dimly aware of people coming out along the street to see what the noise was and of Arthur burying himself in his mother's skirts at the sound, but for those moments until it rested on the slate of the path his whole world was the clock, its smoothness, its scent, and its ticking like blood in his ears.

"Here," he said to Arthur once he had caught his breath. "Come and listen to this." He gripped the boy's arm and pulled him to where Dafydd already had his ear pressed to the clock. He looked up, smiling, and saw Catrin's face. He reached up and took her hand and placed it on the door of the clock. "Feel that," he said. She ran her fingers over the surface lightly, but he placed his hand over hers and pressed it flat. She looked at him for a moment uncertainly and then she too felt the beat of the pendulum and she smiled at him. "It's beautiful," she said, and then frowned quickly, but he leaned across to her and whispered, "You want it. It's yours."

He looked up and saw the carter grinning broadly. Behind him their neighbors were looking on enviously. Thomas suddenly wanted to get rid of the man and to have his front door closed. He straightened up and nodded to the carter. "Shall we get her in then?" But Catrin was after whispering something to him and he turned back to her.

"Just as far as the hallway, mind."

"What?"

She pulled him aside.

"Just let him bring it as far as the hallway. You and Dafydd can manage it from there."

"It's as big as Goliath's coffin and as heavy as if he was in there himself. Why shouldn't he help me with it into the parlour?"

She leaned against him and put her mouth to his ear.

"Look at his shoes," she said. "He's around that horse of his all day long."

"Well, we'll get him to take them off."

"No! I'm not having that man's naked socks in my house. He's not setting foot in my parlour and neither are you for that matter, all hot and sweaty in your dusty, salty clothes."

He looked at her in disbelief.

"Go on. If you're doing it for me, do it my way."

He turned back to the carter, shaking his head like a dog.

When they'd got the clock inside the front door, he motioned the other man to follow him and the two of them squeezed down the hall into the kitchen. Dafydd heard the clank of the big biscuit tin kept on the top shelf of the larder and Catrin had to put a hand on his shoulder to stop him chasing after his father. In a moment the two men, silent now, came out again. She watched them shake hands in the street. "Remember," the carter was saying, "wind every week, oil every month, and she'll never lose a minute. And mind you boys don't run or jump anywhere near her." He nodded toward Catrin, said, "Mrs. Jones," and led his horse away up the street.

Her husband came back to her.

"All right?" she said.

"All done." He smiled so that she would know that he felt fine about giving up the money, although as he stood in the street now he felt light, as if he might float into the sky at any minute. He wanted to look up the street after the carter, but he closed the door. He stared at the clock, and in the gloom of the hall it looked so much heavier than him. He wondered how he would ever lift it.

"So what do you think of your mam's new toy, lads?" he said.

"Great," Dafydd said.

"What about you, Arthur?" But the little boy kept his eyes on the clock and wouldn't look at his father.

"He's not talking to you," Dafydd explained.

"How's that?"

"Because we didn't take him to the beach."

Thomas looked at Catrin. "I tried to explain," she said.

"Haven't we been through this before?" Thomas asked, squatting down to Arthur's level. "You're too big to fit on the bike with Dafydd. I have to take you in turns. It'll be your turn next time. Besides, someone had to stay home with your mother."

Arthur looked at his shoes and pressed closer against his mother. Thomas sighed.

"All right," he said. "Who's for marbles?"

"What about my clock?"

"It's not going anywhere, believe me." He pushed past her toward the kitchen.

They followed him and watched him reach into the pantry for the pail he kept his beer in. There were three bottles bobbing in the cold water, one higher than the others. Thomas pulled out the half-empty one. He swilled the beer around, making the round glass stopper trapped in the neck of the bottle clatter. Then he took a swig. The marble allowed just a mouthful into the neck and then, as he tipped his head back, it fell down, blocking the neck where the glass was pinched, stopping the beer. It took four tips to drain it.

"Very nice," Thomas said, wiping his lips with the back of his hands. Then he got to his feet and stepped into the yard. "Keep back," he told the boys, and he tapped the bottle gently on a stone by the door until it cracked and the marble rolled out. He held it up between his fingers and squinted through it in the evening sun. "Should make a good shooter." He held it out to Arthur. "Quits?" he said. "Friends again?" The little boy nodded solemnly and his father put the marble in his hand. "Go off and see if you can't beat your brother with it."

When he went back in the kitchen, Catrin was filling the washbowl from the bedroom for him, and he followed her upstairs with it. He heard the water slap in the basin and he watched her body move as she carried it before him. She set it on the stand, and he pulled off his shirt and soaped his body while she laid out his Sunday best.

"What about you?" he said when he was finished, and she said, "Help me, then." He went to her and unfastened the buttons of her dress when she turned her back to him.

"Are you pleased with it?" he asked.

"Oh yes," she said. "It looks even finer than in the shop. You're sure you don't mind about it?"

"What's to mind? This is what we've been saving for. No reason we should change our plans." He pulled the dress down off her shoulders.

"How long do you think the strike will last?"

"We'll be back tomorrow. Fellas like me can't take two days of sunshine in a row. It's not healthy. We want to get back underground." He cupped her breasts in his hands and kissed her neck. His hands pushed the dress down to her hips.

"I have to wash," she said.

"You will have to."

"Not now."

"They're happy playing downstairs for once. Come on."

"It's too risky. It's not a good time."

"It's never a good time."

"No," she said. "No. You know we couldn't afford another one now."

He let his hands lie still on her for a moment. His face hardened and he turned away and began to pull on his suit so roughly she feared for the stitching.

"You can't predict," she said as she bent over the basin. "It's not worth the risk. What if this strike goes on longer? You just can't tell."

They came down together in silence, she in her best black dress with the shawl and he in his frock coat and best linen with the new collar cutting into his neck. They were dressed for chapel, which was the only way anyone was allowed into Catrin's parlour.

It was the front room of the house, visible from the street, and as in every house in town it was the show room. The boys stood ready to feast their eyes when their mother opened the door. There was the huge dresser with the best china service stacked high on its shelves. There was the embroidered firescreen with the peacock design that lit up as if it were alive when the fire was going behind it. There were the firm horsehair armchairs and chaise, with the velour covering and the antimacassars draped over the backs and the arms like spiderwebs. And finally, there on the small round table at the window was the glass bell with the stuffed weasel rearing up inside it — their mother's pride and joy. Ever since Mrs. Roberts had started the vogue for such things with her little stuffed canary, no parlour in town was complete without a mounted bird or a rabbit or a fish. The boys were entranced by the weasel, with its bared teeth and glinting glass eyes. They half believed that it, and not their mother at all, would tear them limb from limb if they ever set foot in the parlour without shined shoes.

The new clock would go against the wall by the window, and their mother went over and stood there looking down the street to make sure for the umpteenth time that on their way to the shops or to chapel of a morning, when her parlour got the light, all her neighbors would be able to see in and tell the time by her clock.

Thomas had wrapped his arms around the trunk of the clock and was walking it — tipping it from side to side and rocking it on its base — toward the parlour door. He'd locked the pendulum again, but a dull sound of chimes still accompanied every step.

"Careful," she called. "Oh, careful."

He could already feel the sweat softening his stiff Sunday collar and began to grunt with the effort, but he said nothing.

He took a breather at the door and looked in at his wife, leaning back in the window with her eyes closed.

"You'll need to move Willie the bloody weasel if you want me to get it in there."

Catrin said nothing, just lifted the table and moved it to one side carefully. When she looked back at him, Thomas had started laughing.

"What is it?"

He was standing with his back against the door frame, his head back and his eyes closed, laughing thinly.

"Stop that," she said. "Stop it." But he laughed until it seemed he'd laughed all the breath out of him. Finally only his body shook, soundlessly. Conscious of her position, she stepped away from the window toward him and he opened his eyes.

"You bloody fool," he said. "You little bloody fool."

"Go to your room," she hissed at the boys, and they went at once, Arthur already beginning to cry.

"What do you mean talking to me like that in my own house?"

"It's too damn tall," he said. "The ceiling's too low in here."

She ran to where he was and looked up. On one side of the door frame the hallway ceiling — just the bare boards of the landing, really — was a good six inches higher. The parlour ceiling, plastered and with a gas fitting in the center and a fluted picture rail running around it, was too low for the ornamental crown of the clock.

"You never thought, did you?" he said. "You never

even thought to measure it. It couldn't be grand enough for you."

"What are we going to do?"

He shook his head.

"They'll take it back," she said. "You can find the carter and make him wait until dark and take it back."

"Don't talk daft. They'd have his guts for garters if they thought he'd had the money and given it back to us."

She had begun to cry with frustration and she leaned against him, but he kept his arms at his sides. He started laughing again.

"Do something, then," she said, taking an angry step back. He stared at her for a moment. "Go on!" she shouted. "Do something, if you're so clever."

"Go and clear the kitchen table," he told her, and when she hesitated he grabbed her by the elbows and shoved her down the hall. She stumbled, but didn't turn around. "Go on with you! Light the lamp and pull the curtains when you're done."

He threw himself down on the chaise. It was as firm and spotless as the day he'd bought it nine years earlier. He stretched his legs out on the velour, lay his head back, and stared up at the china he'd never eaten off until he heard her step in the hall.

"Go to the front door," he said. "Call if you see anyone. You wouldn't want the neighbors to know." He followed her out into the hall and she heard him calling, "Dafydd, Arthur, where are you hiding?" In a moment she heard the three of them whispering behind her. Arthur came and stood beside her and took her hand. Then she heard the dull chime of the clock being shifted down the hall, past the parlor and into the kitchen.

"Is there anybody?" he called to her. She looked out the door.

"No one."

He didn't answer, but she heard him grunt as if under a great weight and then the sound of cupboard doors being opened and closed.

"You and Arthur keep a good watch now," he called. Then she heard the sound of the saw. She began on instinct to put her hands to her ears but then let them fall to her sides. Instead, she pulled Arthur to her and lifted him into her arms. Afterwards she heard the sound of movement in the hall again and he called, "One more minute." Then she heard Dafydd in the kitchen making a sound she didn't recognize for a moment. *The broom*, she thought at last. *He's sweeping the floor*.

"We're going out for a few minutes. Stay with your mam, Arthur." She heard the kitchen door open and close.

She walked into the parlour with her eyes down and, still holding the boy in her arms, closed the door and sat on the edge of the sofa. She felt Arthur's fingers on her face, trying to cover her eyes, but she looked anyway. They had left the pinnacle of sawn wood on the table beside the weasel, and she took it and pressed it against her cheek until it was warm and wet, smelling the varnish.

Thomas sat outside the back door in the dusk with a bottle of beer, taking swig after swig until it was empty.

He held it in his hand for a moment and then broke it into the pail. Dafydd watched him silently as he fished out the marble and caught it when Thomas threw it to him. Then he watched him drain the last bottle the same way. After a few minutes Arthur came to the door and said his mother had gone to bed.

"Here." His father broke the bottle and tossed him the last marble. "Let's get you two tucked in." He waited while they used the privy and saw them into their room. Then he went and looked in on the parlour. There was hardly an inch to spare between the top of the clock and the ceiling, and it seemed to hunch in the corner. He went over and opened the glass face and turned the hands until they agreed with his pocket watch. "So long as the bloody thing works," he told himself. He turned the key three times, released the pendulum, and went up to his wife.

He undressed slowly in the darkness and folded the good clothes, patting them lightly to make them fall straight on the horse and wetting his fingers to brush off a little sawdust here and there. Once he put his head to one side and listened and thought he could hear the *chunk* of the pendulum downstairs.

"I'll be careful," he told her, climbing into bed, but she said nothing. "Shh," he said, but the only noise was the sound of the bedsprings.

The next morning the gates were still closed. The men hung about reading the notice from management saying that their services were no longer required. The quarry, it said, would be rehiring men from the end of the month under new terms of employment. Ellis Roberts bustled up before long, and the men who had been talking and horsing around stood up straighter and quieted down, feeling a little awkward before a man who still had a purpose. Ellis nodded to them all and nailed up a notice of his own giving the union's demands: that all men suspended before June 12 should be reinstated; that a committee of elected men and managers assess any request for permission for absence; that the Ascension Day holiday be reinstated. At the bottom, he added in pencil, "That all the men of Bethany quarry be rehired as a body instead of applying individually."

Thomas, with Arthur on his shoulders, stood back from the gates and sent Dafydd to worm his way through the crowd to read the new notice. 123 came up beside him.

"So what is it now?" 123 asked. "A holiday or a strike or a lockout?"

"More time on our hands than we bargained for, anyway," Thomas muttered.

He felt strangely light, even with Arthur on his back, and he didn't want to return home so soon. Catrin had still been in bed beside him when he'd woken that morning, rather than downstairs in the kitchen getting his breakfast. She was sleeping soundly and something about her even breathing made him leave her be and creep downstairs to make his own tea. When he roused the boys he put a finger to his lips and the three of them ate their breakfast in silence. He'd found the key to the clock in the pocket of his trousers as he'd pulled them on and slipped it into one of her slippers under the bed, smiling at the thought of the little cry she'd give when she touched it. Now it was only nine and he didn't want to go back to the house in case she was still sleeping. The thought of her lying there so late was oddly disturbing to him, and yet through some mixture of tenderness and guilt he couldn't bring himself to wake her.

"Want a walk?" he said to 123 as Dafydd came back. The big man nodded and hoisted the boy onto his own broad shoulders. They climbed up the steep embankment to the narrow tracks of the quarry railway. Normally there would have been a heavy traffic of carts loaded with slate from the galleries passing down these lines to the worksheds, and Thomas couldn't help looking over his shoulder from time to time as they walked. After about a mile 123 scrambled down the embankment to a patch of wildflowers. He looked back up at Thomas with a grin and shrugged.

Thomas shook his head, but he gave the boys each a push in the back. "Go and help him." He perched on one of the slate railway ties, fetched his makings out of his pocket, and began to roll a cigarette. "Love is it, then?" he called down to 123.

"Maybe. I like giving her things."

"Get used to it."

"No, I tell you I like it. Makes me feel" — he stretched out his arms — "full."

"You're full of something."

"Don't tell me you've never felt that way about Catrin."

Thomas picked a strand of tobacco off his tongue and got to his feet.

"Well, move yourselves," he called, sliding down to them.

When they passed back by the gates an hour later, the boys were running ahead and each man had a bunch of wildflowers in his hand. Loose knots of workers still hung around chatting.

"You make a lovely couple," someone called, and the crowd laughed. The big man smiled and waved, but Thomas walked on without looking round, his ears burning. "Off courting," 123 called out to them.

"Just remember there's more to it than giving," Thomas said when they came to the turning for the Morris house.

"Such as?"

"Taking, maybe."

"Receiving, you mean. Giving and receiving."

"Call it what you like. How's that make you feel?"

123 paused for a moment, puzzled.

"Full, is it?" Thomas asked. "Or empty?"

But the big man just waved him off.

Outside his own house, there was no sign of the boys, and Thomas knew that Catrin must be awake. He pushed open the kitchen door and went in with the flowers held out before him.

No one went to the beach that day or the next. The men hung around the streets in small groups while the union wrote speeches. They were all dressed in their work clothes because none of them had anything else to wear other than their Sunday best. Rumors flew: that the owners were tunneling through to the quarry from the other side of the mountain to take the slate out from under their noses; that the union had six months of strike pay in the coffers, eight months, a year's worth; that the price of slate had tumbled and the owners didn't mind leaving the quarry unworked for a few weeks; that Mr. Randall, the manager, was taking advantage of the break to find himself a young wife in Chepstow.

"At the rate we're going," Thomas told Catrin, "he'll have time to raise himself a family before he's needed back here." She didn't smile, but he let her be. She hadn't spoken to him, beyond calling him to eat, since the day the clock had arrived. She had thanked him for the flowers, but they had gone straight into a vase in the parlour, where they looked out of place in their brightness, rebuked by the rest of the room. In bed, she had laid herself beside him each night but not touched him once. He had liked to sleep with his arm around her, her back against his stomach and his hand in the warmth beneath her breasts, but now he lay on his back listening to her breathing. He could feel his own resentment rising but had decided to say nothing. Instinctively, he felt the scales slowly tipping. If she kept this behaviour up much longer, she would be in the wrong and he would be the aggrieved one.

On the third day the union called a meeting of the men, and as the *caban* where they were used to meeting was locked behind the gates of the quarry, they asked the Reverend Price if they could use the chapel.

The men filed in past the rows of slate headstones in

the small cemetery and took their accustomed places in their own pews. For a few moments they left the gap between each man where their wives and children would normally sit, but then the press of men from the valley made them bunch up.

Ellis Roberts stood at the front of the chapel with his secretary, Merfyn Hughes. They watched silently as the men took their places, but none of them climbed into the pulpit. Without this signal, the men in the pews kept up their talking until the Reverend Price discreetly stepped into it. Silence fell at once — apart from a few sniggers at a smudge of coal dust on the reverend's bald head — and Ellis Roberts began to speak.

"Men," he said, "I want to begin by reading a lesson." He waved a paper before him and slapped it with his free hand. "It's not Scripture — begging your pardon, Reverend — but you must judge how edifying the matter is. It's the *Report to the Committee of Merionethshire Mines*, and it's not something you might have read in your Tory newspapers. You might say, it's a bit dry and dusty." He cleared his throat. "'It is the finding of this report that the average life expectancy of slate miners in the Merionethshire mines is fifty-four years and ten months, in respect of bad-rock men. Quarrymen may expect, on average, forty-eight years, one month, and slate dressers forty-seven years, six months.'" He paused for a moment. "Our time in this world, men, is limited. All the more reason we should be free to determine how we employ it. One man, as you all know, has already been suspended for attending his own mother's deathbed. Pretty soon we won't be able to get time off for our own funerals." There was a ripple of laughter through the chapel.

"Slate quarrying is not a matter of mere manual labor. It's not for nothing that slate-splitting contends on equal footing with music and poetry at local eisteddfods. If Mr. Randall thinks he can work a quarry on the same principles of government as a dockyard or a brickworks or a cotton factory or pottery or ironworks or coal mine, even, he is greatly mistaken. To bring such a wide-open works as ours under the strict rules of the factories is, I put it to you, rank arrogance."

The speech ended in thunderous applause, Thomas clapping so hard his palms stung and 123 striking his huge hands together like a peal of bells. As the noise died down, Ellis called for questions.

"What's the strike pay to be?" someone shouted. Merfyn Hughes stepped forward and coughed once into his fist.

"Five shillings, sixpence a week, every man," he said, and there was a hush.

Ellis added, "We must prepare ourselves for the longest dispute we can sustain, men. The union will support you, but you must look to yourselves also, especially those with large families. I don't have to tell you that food comes first now. Food is our strength. That means fewer fine clothes for your wives and — something you've heard in this chapel before — less beer for all you men." There was a muttering from the pews at that, and he raised his voice to carry over it. "This is a siege we're living under here. A siege. We're besieging them and they're besieging us. The question is, who can stand it? It would be nice if we could take a leaf out of the reverend's book, here, and march around the quarry blowing trumpets until the management gave in, but we can't count on that. In a siege, everything is turned upside down. Cheap clothes and small portions are what it takes. Poverty is a virtue. The poorer you live today, the longer you live."

Thomas joined the renewed applause but kept his head bowed. Afterwards, he studied his hands in his lap, watching the redness fade. He turned them over, opening and closing his fists, watching the way the bones moved under the skin. Once in a pub in Bangor he'd seen inside a piano, the delicate, precise mechanism of wires and levers. He wondered that he'd never looked at his hands before, though he used them every day, and he found himself staring down the pew at the hands of men, where they lay curled or clenched, still or twitching with impatience.

"How long?" another voice called. "How long will the strike fund last at this rate?"

"Friend. Four hundred yards up the street here is our enemy. Every word I speak today will carry that far even if I were to whisper it. Therefore, I ask you, would it be wise for me to answer that question? But I will tell you this. We should give thanks, every one of us, that our homes hereabouts are leased from farmers and not from the mine owners. That is a strong enough base, our homes, to support many months, many years of struggle."

A final round of applause broke out.

"Ha," said 123, leaning into Thomas. "Same as the bloody army. Hurry up and wait."

The following day the management posted a new notice on the quarry gates. Owing to the temporary depression in the slate trade, the quarry, it said, would not be rehiring for sixteen weeks. Dewi Parry, the foreman, still went to work every day, and two constables stood at the gate at all hours.

Many of the men drifted away, some as far as Liverpool, others only to family farms in the valley below, in search of work. Those left played football daily with teams of twenty or thirty, hacking the ball across the sloping hillsides until they realized that it was making them too hungry. William Williams, the publican, had to move his dartboard onto the outside wall of the inn because of the crush of men waiting their turn to play. "None of you buggers buy a drop to drink anymore," he complained, "and I can't stand to have you lurking around, licking your lips every time I sell a pint." On sunny days he even let them carry out the huge billiard table. They would rest it in a field and spend hours levelling it in place before they could play. Each new player, coming down from among the crowd watching the game on the hillside, would carry, in addition to his chalk, his plumb line to check the lie of the table between shots.

Thomas hung around the house for a few days, uncertain of how to fill his time. Catrin was speaking to him now, but more out of irritation at having him underfoot than forgiveness. He sat at the kitchen table and watched her work until she grew exasperated. "If you're so fascinated, you do it," she'd tell him, holding out the rag she was polishing with or the knife for paring potatoes, but if he reached out to take it she would snatch it back with a look that made him feel like a fool. One morning she caught him on aching knees, cleaning out the grate. He had hoped to surprise her, but she had pulled him up roughly. "Where's your pride?" she had hissed, and he'd been too shocked to speak before she had turned and gone.

He tried to play with the boys, but after the novelty of having him home had worn off, they seemed to prefer to spend their time with Catrin. Perhaps, he thought, this was how it had always been between them when he was out at work. It made him sad, the thought of this secret life of theirs. He would walk in on them playing a game or reading together. Catrin would look up at him and put the book down and ask him what he wanted, but if he told her to go on reading, she would get up and busy herself, as if she felt she should be working in front of him. He felt the eyes of the boys on him and he would make some excuse, say he was tired, although from what he couldn't imagine, and go upstairs and stretch himself out on the bed. She had taken to using the parlour more, perhaps because there were now four of them about the house all day, and she would read in there often. She said the light was better, but he wondered if it wasn't because she knew he felt uncomfortable in there. He would lie above, listening to her voice through the floorboards. She read softly and for the most part he couldn't make out the words, could only follow the story by the boys' exclamations and their laughter, but he listened to the tone of her voice and tried to imagine what she was feeling, until the clock's chimes called her back to her chores.

He usually lent a hand on his uncle's farm in the valley at harvest time, and now, though it was still summer, he started spending his days there doing odd jobs, rebuilding field walls, trapping rabbits. He brought the farmer or perhaps his cousin up the hill with him on evenings when there were billiards. When 123 Davies wasn't courting, he kept a place in line for him, and when it was Thomas's turn he would wager a day's free labour on the farm against eggs or milk. It was said that slate miners had an affinity for the game of billiards, because of the slate beds beneath the green baize of the tables, and whenever Thomas won, which was often, he would shake hands with his uncle or cousin and say gravely that the slate had favoured him. Out of any dozen eggs he always gave three to 123 Davies. "Two for your breakfast, one for your mother," he'd say, and the big man would clap him on the back. Catrin would take the remaining nine and hardboil them all. Often she would give three each to him and the boys and say she wasn't hungry. On other occasions, when she was angry, she would gobble down three herself in quick succession while they watched her.

"You'll make yourself sick," Thomas told her, but he said nothing when he heard her retching in the mornings.

SEPTEMBER

At the end of four months no one had seen Randall, the manager, since the Ascension Day holiday. The common joke, as they waited outside the quarry to see what the company would do now, was that he was searching far and wide for a bride, from Chepstow across the border to Bristol and Bath and Cheltenham. "Someplace where they haven't seen a man in a while," Ellis Roberts said with a smile, and the people nearby laughed. A crowd of almost four hundred, including women and children, was waiting to see who, if anyone, would reapply to the mine. The union had issued no special instruction to stop anyone from trying to return to work; the crowd was just curious to see what kind of man could do such a thing.

The three Evans brothers, drunkards who lived on the outskirts of the town, had been bragging that they would break the strike, but no one seriously expected them to appear. The back pew in chapel was kept empty for them to slip into on Sunday mornings after a rough Saturday night, which they did more often than not. When they did saunter into sight at the bottom of the street, the crowd greeted them with hoots of derision.

"*Cynffonwyr!*" they called. "Monkeys! Show us your tails!"

Bob Evans, the eldest, grinned and reached for his fly, which caused more laughter. He began to walk with his brothers toward the gate, and the crowd parted before them, chattering excitedly.

"Nothing but a sideshow," the union chairman said

calmly. "When they see that these are the best fellows they can get to break the strike, we'll be back in the quarry in a week."

Thomas put Arthur on his shoulders, but Dafydd complained from the ground until 123 swung him up in turn. "See the monkey-men?" he cried to the boy, while his own eyes sought out Mair standing with her father on the other side of the street. Catrin stood silently beside her husband with her head down, holding people off her stomach with her hands.

The Evanses reached the gate, where Dewi Parry waited with the same four constables as before.

"Let us through," Bob shouted. He pressed his face to the bars and bellowed, "Let us through." The foreman recoiled a step. "We'd like a job," Bob explained meekly, and the crowd roared with laughter.

"Is this a joke?" the foreman asked.

Bob lunged at him, thrusting his arm through the bars, trying to grab the other man until a constable's truncheon cracked him on the elbow and he jumped back, howling, into the arms of his brothers. The crowd laughed again.

"There are no jobs here," Dewi Parry called, and that quietened them.

"You wouldn't know a real job if it came up and bit you in the arse," someone called from the crowd.

"They're all taken," the foreman shouted back. The crowd was momentarily stilled, and in the silence that followed a new sound could be made out, the sound of boots. Behind them, coming up the hill, were Mr. Randall, a line of constables, and a body of men they'd never seen before. The constables swished their truncheons through the air before them like scythes and the crowd fell back to let them past.

"Who are they?" Dafydd asked, but they heard Ellis Roberts's voice over all of theirs, shouting for quiet.

"Listen," he shouted, "listen!" For the new men were talking among themselves, looking from side to side at the quarrymen.

"It's English," Catrin said quietly.

"I know that accent," 123 shouted. "They're Cornishmen. They're bloody Cornishmen."

The men had been inactive for so long that the Cornishmen were just what they needed. Ellis Roberts called a meeting appealing for order, but at the appointed time the chapel was still only half full and he went out onto the steps and tried to talk to the groups of men loitering in the street. He called them to him, but they'd have none of him and he was reduced to speaking to their backs.

"Remember, friends," he called. "There is a peculiar suitability in Welshmen, an innate genius, for the treating of slate. What do Cornishmen know about slate? Blacklegs are nothing. All we have to fear are scabs." But they weren't having any of it.

Ellis watched the street empty and pushed his hands into his pockets, looking for his pipe. He struck the match with his fingernail and sat back on the chapel steps and inhaled deeply. He used to fill a pipe before a blasting, after the warning gun, while the men climbed the narrow ladders out of the quarry. He would sit and smoke and watch birds fly across the pit below him until he was the only man left on the face, and then he would light the homemade straw fuse. He used black powder for the main charge — packed into a hole he'd bored in the rock with a long iron awl called a jumper — because it split the rock, finding the natural faults without blowing it to bits. He could sit on a ledge not ten feet above the blasting cap and feel nothing but a bracing gust of wind as slabs of slate twenty feet long slid away below him. "A controlled explosion," he whispered to his wife whenever she clutched him in her sleep. "Controlled, see."

This evening he knocked out his pipe before it was half smoked and stepped back inside the chapel.

123 called for Thomas at dusk.

"You're too late for supper," Catrin said, looking up from the sink as her brother came into the kitchen. The big man looked confused for a moment.

"We're just off after a bit of exercise," Thomas told her, pulling on his coat and pushing the big man toward the door.

"Oh, aye. And maybe a pint," 123 added. Thomas could have kicked him.

"I'd have thought you'd have better things to spend your money on."

"It's his money," Thomas said quietly. "He earned it."

Catrin just stared at him until he looked away.

"And how's Mair Morris these days, Roy?" she asked. "Have the two of you set a date yet?"

The big man blushed.

"Come on," Thomas said angrily. He snatched up his umbrella and went out the door, but Catrin caught her brother's arm and Thomas had to wait a few minutes, tapping the point of his umbrella on the path impatiently.

"We'll be late," he said when the big man finally joined him in the street.

"Just a minute," 123 said, and he stooped beside the wall to retrieve a long, thin bundle wrapped loosely in rags. Thomas caught a dull glint from one end. "Didn't want to bring it in with me," 123 said apologetically as he slipped it inside his coat.

The quarrymen met the blacklegs before the gates that same evening, with not an official or a constable anywhere to be seen, and fell upon them at once.

They carried their umbrellas and billiard cues and mallets, but it was the sight of 123 Davies with his Zulu spear that made the burly Cornishmen turn tail. Half of them fled over the hill behind the quarry and the other half back into the workings, where they were chased up and down the ladders and through the galleries until they collapsed breathless in the darkness, where their panting gave them away. Their arms and legs tied, their shirts filled with slate, they were thrown into the backs of the wagons sent to take them down to town. "Back to your tin mines and your clotted cream," the quarrymen called, and they snapped their umbrellas open and closed to scare the horses. A relay of lads, Dafydd among them, followed the carts downhill, screaming and throwing slate chips at the horses' rumps to make them run faster.

That night the men occupied the quarry. They lifted the huge gates off their hinges and carried them away to the grass hillside, and boys climbed on and rode them through the long grass like toboggans into the valley, scattering sheep in their path. On their way back up they set light to gorse bushes behind them — lighting twisted up newspapers, kicking a hole in the bush, and pushing the paper inside — until the night crackled with fire.

The men went to their caban as usual and brewed their old tea — the leaves and water and sugar all thrown in the kettle together and left on the fire for thirty minutes. They drew up the old smooth benches and shook their heads over the state of tools and machinery long idle. They sent for the union chairman to make a speech, but it was the preacher who came instead and sat with them at the whitewood table until dawn, reading Scripture. In the lamplight, it was observed that there was a distinctly blue shadow, the purple of wet slate, over his ears and encircling his head.

Thomas's part in all this was to help find the last Cornishman — a boy so afraid of being alone in the dark that they found him by his sobbing. He clung to the ladder he was on and they had to pry his fingers loose to pull him up.

123 stayed by Thomas's side throughout the fight. "Catrin asked me to keep an eye out for you, didn't she?" he said sheepishly when Thomas asked him what he

thought he was doing. "Ha-bloody-ha," Thomas told him.

They stood back and watched as others lifted the gates down and then sat and drank tea until dawn. At last Thomas slapped the big man on the knee and told him he was off home. When he came down the hill to the house, the village was silent and full of smoke from the fires. He stayed close to the wall on the High and his footsteps sounded muffled. He found Catrin already at work in the yard, despite the smoke. She had the hearth rug out on the line and was beating it hard.

"Hey," he said from the kitchen door. "Hey. D'you want to wake the dead? There's people trying to sleep this morning."

"There's people" — she struck the rug again, without turning — "should have honest jobs to go to."

"That's another lot of noise you best keep to yourself," he said.

"Then leave me be," she said. "Fetch your own breakfast since you've so much time to go gallivanting."

"That's right," he said tiredly. He could feel the effects of the tea wearing off.

"Don't worry about feeding the boys," she said. "They're still sleeping. Arthur was so frightened by all the noise he came in and slept with me. Then we were both woken up by his brother coming in at the dead of night."

"What dead of night?"

She turned and put her hands on her hips.

"Four o'clock. I heard it strike in the parlor."

"You probably heard him going to the privy."

"He didn't come back from the privy black with soot, did he? He was out on that mountain lighting gorse bushes with my matches all night."

"Don't take on so. It's only a gorse bush, woman."

She came close to him.

"Your uncle has already been up here to see about work this morning. He said to tell all you fellows not to come down the valley for a day or two. One of his neighbor's sheep got out of the pen and burned up last night."

He looked at her and there were tears on her face and he tried to pull her to him. She stiffened, and he had to lean over her. He gripped her gently around the shoulders and held his breath when he felt his sharp belt buckle touch her stomach.

"I'll talk to him," he whispered, smelling the dust of the rug in her hair. "There's no harm done yet," and she said, "I wanted to go out to find him, but I couldn't leave Arthur and I didn't know where you were."

"There now," he said. "Bear up. It'll all be over soon. They'll come to terms now."

The men slept most of that day and it was only the women, from their parlour windows, who saw the departures: Ellis Roberts, with only a sack on his back, his wife with her stuffed bird in her hands and the children with a china dog under each arm; Merfyn Hughes, in his Sunday suit, pushing his velocipede. Those with houses at the edge of town said they shook hands briefly and then took different paths over the hill behind the quarry, Hughes carrying his bicycle on his back over the rough ground.

The chapel bell was what woke them in the late afternoon, and the Reverend Price who broke the news to them that the strike fund was as good as exhausted. It was a terrible blow, but the reverend stared down from his pulpit with bright, darting eyes.

"Do not think ill of those who have left," he cried. "They fought with themselves to tell you the truth, but held back for fear they would also be telling the enemy. They feared to strengthen him in his conviction to beat you down. I tell you this now, because it is my belief that we will win out not with money but with strength of purpose, with honest pride, and with faith.

"The path to Canaan," he intoned over the murmuring in the chapel, "throughout the ages, has led through desert, chaos, and pain. The Lord tests us only to make better men of us when we step forth from the furnace. If but one man be purified by the fire, it will not have been set in vain. I say unto you, do not go back into Egypt, my people. Do not give in to temptation. You will be destroying the slate works of creation if you give way. Carry on, I say. Carry on the good fight, for the Lord *will* provide."

Thomas and Catrin sat in silence. He would have liked to take her hand, to comfort her or himself, but when he looked in her lap he saw her hands together, as if in prayer. They looked so composed he did not like to disturb them, and he slid his own hands beneath his thighs. Afterwards, they filed out into the street with the rest of the villagers without a word. There, apart from a few scattered curses against the union men, the talk was of nothing but the thin circle of hair — for hair it certainly was, those in the front pews insisted — that had appeared above the reverend's ears and temples. "It goes all the way round," those who had lingered to watch him leave affirmed. It seemed natural after the failure of their elected representatives to put their faith in a man so trustworthy and so blessed.

There was an uneasy calm in the village in the days after the rout of the Cornishmen. No constables were sent and the foreman, Dewi Parry, did not appear for work each day. The harvest was in on the farms by this time and there was less and less need for casual labour, so the men lounged around the streets and stretched out on the hillsides, enjoying the last fine days of autumn.

They began to complain about their bowels running more slowly than usual. They muttered about it darkly in small groups before chapel and in the darker recesses of the pub. Some put it down to the shortage of food. Their bodies were retaining what they ate longer to keep them from hunger, they claimed. Others suggested that they were losing their regularity because they no longer spent hours each day sitting on cold slate. In their parlours, in more polite company, their wives noticed that they hadn't pared their nails in weeks and some that rust was forming on their husbands' razors. The men just rubbed their hands over their chins and shrugged, while their wives laughed and said how much they preferred it. Children, it was said, had stopped growing, and indeed in the schoolroom where heights were recorded each fortnight it was noticed that no child had grown for several months. Men who had been away in the valleys working through the summer came back looking like giants.

Thomas himself could not recall the last time he had had a bowel movement. "I can't even remember the last time I had a good fart," he told 123 one day. At night he grumbled to Catrin. "It's not natural," he said. "It's not comfortable."

"Go to sleep," she said. "Don't worry about it."

"What about you?" he said. "Any problems?"

She rolled over and looked at him piercingly in the gloom. "Such as?" she said, but he couldn't bring himself to ask.

"You know," he said.

She turned away from him and plumped her pillow roughly. Then she curled herself into a ball around her belly, with her back to him. "I've forgotten," she said over her shoulder. "Better things to worry about, I expect. Go to sleep."

"What about the boys?" he insisted.

"The boys are fine." She yawned. "Don't worry about them. They'll shoot up into men one of these days and surprise you."

With Hughes, the schoolteacher, gone, Dafydd's days were free, and Thomas tried to teach him some quarrying. Since the night of the mountain fire, Catrin had become ever more attentive to the boys, letting them nestle against her as she read to them, stroking their hair with her free hand. "Mollycoddling," Thomas called it, and when she ignored him he nicknamed the boys "Agnes" and "Daphne." After all, he told himself, Dafydd would be twelve soon, old enough to become a *rubbler* when the quarry reopened. He brought back some small pieces of rubbish slate from the waste hill behind the mine and showed Dafydd how to handle a real chisel until Catrin complained of the noise in her kitchen. Then he began taking the boy up to the waste hill, to do their work there. 123 Davies, who often hung about his old workplace, found them there and begged Thomas to show him how to split slate too.

"If you think you can take the time off courting," Thomas told him.

"From the longest courtship in history?" the big man grumbled. "I reckon so."

So the three of them spent the fortnight after the defeat of the Cornishmen gripping slates between their knees, taking turns with the hammer and chisel.

It took ten days for 123 Davies to give up his second attempt at becoming a quarryman proper. Dafydd, after a slow beginning, had just split a slate so thin you almost felt you could see through it. "Make a good writing slate, will that," his father told him.

"Ha!" the big man exclaimed when the piece he was working with broke apart in his hands. He was using the heavy wooden mallet known as a Big Rhys and he shook it in the air looking for something to strike. "Ah, to hell with it," he said and made to fling the tools into the quarry below them.

"Hey!" Thomas cried, but 123 was already smiling. He handed over the tools.

"Better keep those safe," he said. "Never know when you'll be needing them."

Thomas studied the tools in his hands. He wiped the wooden handles with a rag and then rolled them up in it.

"You shouldn't give up," he said.

"Ah, what do I need with a hobby?"

"Needn't be a hobby if you kept at it."

"Careful. You're sounding like Mother now," 123 said.

Thomas looked at him and the big man met his eyes. Then, very deliberately, 123 put three fingers in his mouth and sucked them where the chisel had grazed them. The boy laughed.

"Funny, eh? D'you think that's funny? Do you want to race me?"

"Where?" the boy said.

"Up here." He gestured up the sloping slate pile behind him. Dafydd looked at his father.

"His mother'd kill me if she knew."

"Chicken. Come on! I'll take the both of you. What are you, mice or men?"

He stood and hefted a slab of slate in his hand.

"When this hits the tin roof of Dewi Parry's office, all right? Ready? Steady?" He heaved the slate into the quarry pit below them and in a second they were all rushing up the slope of the hill.

The big man launched himself upward with great thrusts of his legs and soon left them in his wake. Then there was no coming back at him, because he was above them and any slates he dislodged came sliding past them and made their footing slippery. Long before they reached the top, where 123 waited, Thomas had taken Dafydd's hand to help him up.

"It's like climbing a mountain of shit," 123 yelled down. "You take two steps back for each one up. Did I ever tell you that story? About the man who climbs the mountain of shit to get the one red rose at the top?"

"No," Thomas said breathlessly. "What about him?"

"Lost his bloody sense of smell, didn't he?"

By the time they reached the top, 123 Davies was looking past them down the hillside. They sat carefully so as not to slide down any farther and panted beside him for a moment.

"Tell me, Dafydd," he said. "What do you see below the village?"

They looked where he was pointing. There was dust rising above the drystone walls of the lanes and every so often a flash of something. Thomas watched for a minute and then looked out farther down the valley, searching for his uncle's farm and then the road to the sea. He'd heard you could see Ireland on a clear day, but the sun on the water dazzled him and he couldn't make out any shadow of land at the horizon.

"They look good," 123 said. "Dragoons, I think. Proud of their marching."

Thomas looked down into the village and saw the head of the column coming up High Street toward the quarry. He counted twenty rows of men, three abreast, with two officers on horseback. The flash they had seen above the lanes was the bayonets of the troops. 123 jumped to his feet and began to bound down the slate, sinking into the loose chips and sliding a few yards, then leaping on again. Thomas kept a firm hold of Dafydd's hand and they picked their way down gingerly. As it was, the boy managed to rip the knees out of his breeches. "There'll be hell to pay at home," Thomas said gently.

Troops were running through the street as they made for the house, but the soldiers took no notice of the man and boy. Thomas saw them break down Ellis Roberts's front door and post a guard. Then as he neared home he saw another patrol escorting Dewi Parry. The foreman was red in the face from hurrying with the troops, and he held a stack of letters in his hands. Thomas watched him stop at the Morris house and knock. When Cyril Morris, Mair's father, answered, he handed over a letter and then trotted off with the soldiers. Catrin was looking out for them from the parlour, and he was shocked to see her there with her apron still covered in flour.

The next day was Sunday, and one by one men and women in their best clothes stepped onto the street. They left all their children inside. They nodded to their neighbours and began to make their way to chapel, walking arm in arm in silence.

In chapel, the reverend, now sporting an almost full head of hair, called for everyone who had received a letter to stand, and the congregation scrutinized carefully the twenty men, Cyril Morris among them, who got hesitantly to their feet. Then, from somewhere at the back of the hall, someone said, "It's the band," and people looked at the faces again and nodded yes. They were all members of the quarry brass band.

The reverend read one of the letters aloud in English while the men and women tried to puzzle out the ominous-sounding words. Then he read it in Welsh. The company, which had provided the instruments, required the men of the band to return them forthwith. They were held only so long as the men were employees of the mine and, since the termination of said employment, reverted to the company. A magistrate's order had been obtained, the letter said, and the men would be expected to return the instruments in good order, no later than the following morning, on pain of prosecution.

The reverend explained that it had been revealed to him in a dream that the men might replenish the strike fund by sending their band around the country to play at fairs and factories. But now the enemy, in league with the archvillain himself, had anticipated this divine plan. When he exhorted them to pray for guidance and fell to his knees, no one thought to point out that the very same plan had brought the strikers of Corliss almost five thousand pounds during a dispute ten years earlier. They only had eyes for his head bent toward them, and while he prayed, all the men and women in the chapel murmured the words of the prayer with their heads up and their eyes open, staring at the diminishing bald spot on the reverend's crown. As he prayed, he rocked gently to relieve the pressure on his aging knees, and the light from the high windows slid back and forth across this spot.

"Once more, my Lord," the reverend cried, "you burden us. But be the burden ever so weighty, the men will bear it." Thomas heard Catrin panting with the effort of kneeling, and he helped her quickly to her feet —

despite her angrily trying to shake him off — before anyone noticed.

"What we are asked for," the reverend told them when he stood before them once more, "we shall surrender. And in our surrender make ourselves strong."

The next morning was the last day of September. The strikers gathered in the High Street behind the band, and on a signal from the reverend the men began to march toward the quarry. No one spoke, and the only sounds were the tramp of boots and the rattle of instruments. Women and children — Catrin and the boys included, despite Thomas's forbidding it — brought up the rear.

The dragoons were already drawn up in rows before the empty gateposts of the quarry, the caban and the workshops behind them. An officer on horseback rode along the face of his men, and a burly sergeant stood to one side of the rank. Mr. Randall and Dewi Parry stood a little behind the troops, in the lee of one of the gateposts.

The band drew up about ten yards before the soldiers and stood silently while the rest of the crowd fanned out around them. 123, beside Thomas, was trying to catch Cyril Morris's eye and give him the thumbsup. But Mair's father, looking pale and sweaty in the grip of his tuba, couldn't take his eyes off the soldiers.

The captain of dragoons wheeled his horse to face them and waited for the crowd to settle. He pulled a notice from his tunic and began to unfold it. "The Riot Act," 123 whispered to Thomas. Once it was read, the crowd would be obliged to disperse immediately or be made to disperse forcibly. The men put their instruments to their lips. The captain cleared his throat and the band began to play.

The sudden noise, especially as the men had not practiced for six months and were badly out of tune, set the captain's horse rearing, and while he was too fine a horseman to lose control, he had to let the notice fall from his hand. It fluttered to the ground, and 123 ran forward and snatched it up in his fist. The captain, who had only one copy and couldn't hope to recite the act from memory, signaled his men forward. It took six of them almost two full bars of music to pin the big man down. The band played on, waiting for a signal from the reverend, who could only rub the stubble forming on his chin and look in vain for the collapse of the quarry walls. The sergeant of dragoons stepped forward and picked up a rifle dropped by one of his men in the scuffle. For perhaps a moment more the instruments of the band and the bayonets and bandoliers and brass buttons of the dragoons caught the light, and then a rifle butt was raised and snapped down on 123's closed fist.

The band stopped, and they could hear the big man's sobs. A dragoon knelt and wrenched open the broken hand. It was empty. The rifle butt was raised again, and this time when it came down on the other fist, the sound of breaking bone could be heard all the way down High Street. The second hand was empty, and a moment later 123 began to retch up pieces of chewed paper.

As if on a signal, the street was filled with running men pouring back down the street. Instruments clanked in the dust, and only the reverend walked slowly downhill, stroking his light beard.

Catrin, shielding her boys in a doorway, watched her husband swept by in the crowd but did not call out. She saw him lose his hat, the bowler caught by a gust, bouncing off someone's shoulder before it vanished down a crack in the crowd. Thomas did not even turn. She saw it after the crowd had passed, lying in the street, its crown flattened and creased. The reverend, pausing beside it, shook his head. "Such a shame," he called to her, stooping and taking the ruined hat in his hands and turning it over. He pushed the crown out, smoothed it into a semblance of its former shape, and held it out to her. "Here," he said, and after a moment she pushed Dafydd forward. "Thank you," she cried as Dafydd took the hat. The reverend smiled, the teeth white in his black beard. He watched the boy walk back to his mother, but as she stepped out of the doorway and took the hat into her hands, his expression changed. His lips closed and he turned and hurried downhill. Catrin, the hat against her stomach, watched him go.

OCTOBER

It didn't matter that 123 Davies had never been able to split a slate straight in his life: the message to the quarrymen was clear. The memory of that sound made grown men wince, and the sight of 123 about town brought tears to their eyes. Many of them walked around with their fists clenched in their pockets for weeks, not out of anger but from an instinct to protect their precious hands.

The big man himself took it quietly, although his anger grew the longer his hands took to heal. He learned to balance his too-small bowler hat on his head and spent his days walking around the town with his bandaged hands behind his back and his head held high but very still on his massive neck. It was a point of pride with him in case he should meet any dragoons out patrolling the streets. "It wouldn't do for a guardsman to be seen bareheaded before those swine," he told Thomas confidentially. Whenever a patrol passed him, he would walk toward them with his head up, his eyes blazing, and the veins in his neck bulging like cords. His forehead would buckle in thick fleshy creases. It must have given the young soldiers a sense of his pent-up rage, because not one of them would meet his eye.

In the knots of men at the streetcorners there was some talk about returning to work, but the figure of 123 stalking stiff-backed through the town invariably quelled it. Everyone knew that whatever the outcome of the strike now, he was a marked man. He had been singled out on the day his hands were broken. No quarry in Wales would hire him again. With all his strength, he'd be lucky to find any job above that of a labourer. No one was surprised when he broke off his engagement. People said they could hear Mair from the street sobbing in her room, but Cyril Morris didn't even ask 123 for an explanation. To Thomas, he just shook his head. "It's too bad. She doesn't know it yet, but he's done right by her."

One evening as 123 and Thomas walked through the

square they met a patrol led by the sergeant who had broken 123's hands. By now the villagers knew his name was Briggs and that he often led the dusk patrol himself. If he did so, he invariably ended it at the doors of William Williams's public house, which the dragoons had pretty much made their own. They spent freely, drinking down pint after pint under the thirsty gaze of the few quarrymen with money enough to nurse one or two drinks all night. Of them all, Briggs was the worst. He it was who had insisted that Williams bring in first the dartboard and then the billiard table "for his paying customers." Williams didn't like to be told his own business, or to be reminded of his charity to the quarrymen, which slightly embarrassed him, but he was glad of an excuse to bring his table indoors. At the end of September a couple of blazing hot days had dried out the nap so much that it stood on end and made the table run slower and slower. Balls that should have flown into the pockets hung on the lip and cost quarrymen a couple of games against farmers who couldn't believe their luck. "Look at her, boys. She's running like molasses. I can't leave her out here," Williams cried as he hauled the table in. The beer-laden air soon flattened the nap.

Sergeant Briggs was an appalling player, the worst anyone in the village could remember. He had no feel for the game, no touch, and his only pleasure in playing seemed to be the crack of the balls smacking into one another. The watching quarrymen couldn't contain their disapproval. "Leave it be if you don't want to play properly," they called. "Move over for them as knows the game." Briggs, not understanding a word of the Welsh, would only straighten up from each dreadful shot and walk slowly around the table to where his drink lay. He'd lift it, call out, "Your health, you pagans," and drain it in one. The watching men would gradually fall silent as they saw another glass slowly empty.

In the dusk, Thomas realized too late who it was leading the patrol. He put his hand on 123's arm, but the big man shook him off roughly, weaving a little in the street with his eyes rolled back in his head to keep his hat balanced. Once he had it under control he marched on, with Thomas at his side almost running to keep up, whispering all the time, as he might to one of the cows in his uncle's shed, "Steady now, steady." The patrol was coming down one of the side streets that led into the square and was made up of ten men, two abreast. Trotting down the middle of the lane, their brass buckles jingling in the evening air, the dragoons took up so much space that the quarrymen would have to turn sideways to let them pass. Thomas tried to cut 123 off, angling his own path across that of the other, but the big man strode on resolutely, and Thomas had to scurry to get out of his way. In the end, just as a collision seemed inevitable, the sergeant raised his hand and stopped the patrol. The tramp of their boots rang on in the air for a moment, as if the sound of them had marched on a couple more steps. Then silence.

Briggs, a florid man with a broad moustache that joined his sideburns, stepped forward and looked 123 up and down. The striker's bandaged hands shone in the twilight.

"Heard you was a soldier," the sergeant said firmly.

His little black eyes stared into 123's for a second more, and then he stepped back and gave a little nod. "Good show," he said and looked at 123 expectantly. They stood like this for ten seconds and then twenty, until Thomas could see the eyes of the dragoons in the front rank begin to roam.

"What are you doing?" he hissed in Welsh. "Nod back and let's be on our way."

"I can't," the big man replied carefully. "I'll lose me hat."

Thomas looked over and saw that the bowler was already perched at a rakish but perilous angle on the big man's head. More seconds passed.

"Do something," 123 whispered. "It's slipping." Thomas looked again and saw that the big man had begun to dip one shoulder and lean back to keep the hat balanced, jutting his belly out aggressively. The sergeant followed Thomas's gaze and began to lean to one side himself, searching 123's face with a look of puzzlement. Behind him the patrol began to jingle lightly in the darkness, and as if reminded of their existence, the sergeant turned and gestured the men to part. He looked at 123 again, gave a deep ceremonial bow, and waved him through the rank of men. The big man walked on slowly, with his head cocked stiffly to one side, while Thomas, surrounded by dragoons, whispered hoarsely from behind him, "Move yourself, man."

The sergeant watched them, expecting at any minute that the big striker would turn and acknowledge him, but he walked awkwardly to the head of the lane with his stocky friend and they vanished without a backward glance. The sergeant waved the line of dragoons to close up and walked them slowly through the rest of their patrol to the door of the pub.

Once round the corner, 123 pushed Thomas to one side and whispered hoarsely, "Catch my hat."

He sighed contentedly as Thomas lifted it straight and resettled it, but where it had slid over his brow a ridge of muscle would not relax. Thomas pinched it.

"Can you feel that?" he said, but the big man didn't say anything. Thomas pinched again, hard, but the muscle still wouldn't give, and he was happy to stop, because the flesh between his fingers felt like old rope.

When 123 finally mastered the trick of keeping his hat in place, he became more himself again, although not before Thomas found him once stopped dead in the street, staring down at his hat where it had slipped off, unable to retrieve it, spitting with rage. After that, if Thomas couldn't walk with him himself — and he spent more time around the house now — he sent Dafydd along. They made a strange pair, the big man with his stiff carriage and the boy with his father's beaten old bowler hat hanging over his ears. Thomas had taken it back when Catrin had offered it to him, but he couldn't bear to wear it.

The muscle in 123's brow never did relax. His mother tried ointments and poultices, but Catrin ran a finger over the hard ridge and shuddered. Even after the bandages came off, it was clear that 123 would carry his frown for the rest of his life. He let children balance pennies and pencils against his forehead and laughed along with them, but none of the men laughed easily around him, not in the presence of that frown.

NOVEMBER

In the fifth month of the lockout, the company posted a notice offering a new wage and a new contract for returning men. Mr. Randall nailed up a list of factory regulations from a cotton mill in Manchester to show how lenient the quarry terms were. In ones and twos, men — mostly from the valley — did begin to drift back. A patrol of dragoons circled the village each morning, meeting the returning workers at their doors and accompanying them to work.

It was a soldier in this patrol who insulted Martha Thomas one morning when she was out washing her stoop. She was on her hands and knees in the street with a bucket beside her, both hands working the old scrub brush against the slate of the step, when the patrol went by. She said nothing, kept her back to them, but heard the laughter behind her. She went at once to the reverend, who called the men together in the chapel. There was much debate when it was found that Martha did not actually know what had been said.

"How'd she know it was an insult, then?" Bob Evans wanted to know.

"There is the matter of the laughter," the reverend said. He had by this time sent Martha to her bed, but her husband, Robbie Thomas, spoke up for her. "She could tell, man. People know it when they're being laughed at, whatever the language. She was on her knees, with her back to them, and she could still tell. It's instinct, man."

The image of Martha on her knees, bent over her step, gave the men pause for thought.

"Maybe he said she had a fat arse," Bob offered, and the chapel burst into laughter, despite the reverend's efforts to shout it down.

Robbie Thomas got slowly to his feet and the laughter wore itself out into isolated coughing.

"I'll go by myself, then. And let all of you go alone if it's your wife the next time." He made his way slowly to the door and the men looked at one another. Nodding among themselves, they got to their feet and filed out after Robbie.

At the edge of the square he turned around and the whole crowd looked behind them. "Get back, then!" Robbie shouted. "I'll do my duty by my wife without the help of a mob." But when he set off again they sauntered after him. They could see Robbie's neck going red from twenty yards back and they nudged each other. "The English better watch it," they said. "They'll not know what hit 'em."

Long before they reached the quarry, however, they saw white-clad figures emerge from between the gateposts and walk down the High toward them. It was the women of the town, each still in her apron. Grim-faced, they walked down to where the men had stopped in their tracks, and when they reached them they kept walking. Here and there individual men saw their own wives and ran to catch hold of them and find out what was going on. Thomas made out Catrin's head bobbing along among the rest and fought his way through to her. He called her name, but she didn't stop, and he had to fall in beside her or lose her in the crowd of women.

"What's going on?" he said. "What have you all been up to?"

"Just to see the sergeant about his men. We told him about Martha and pointed the man out and now the sergeant will deal with him."

Thomas tried to catch her hand, but she pulled free and swung it beside her all the way home. Only inside was he able to make her stand still for a minute. He looked at the apron tied tightly over her belly and pushed his hand into the pocket at the front of it. One by one he drew out six smooth stones.

"What were these for?" he said, holding them under her nose and shaking them so that they clacked against one another.

"We'd have used them if we had to," she said. "We weren't afraid. Someone had to do something. Where were you men?"

She made to pass him, but he put a hand on her shoulder. He laid the stones down on the kitchen table and slid the empty hand into the warm apron pocket again.

"It's empty," she said. But he was silent and only kept his hand there, open over her belly. She made a soft noise for a moment and then straightened up. "Gerroff," she said, and reached up to loosen the ties of the apron around her neck. She stepped back out of it and he had to clench the material in a fist to stop it sliding to the floor.

"Don't you think I know?" he said to her.

She ran water into the black kettle, letting the water roar against the metal sides.

"Don't you?" he shouted.

She set the kettle down in the sink and shut off the tap and walked past him to the stairs. He watched her back and went after her. On the stairs he heard her running and he called, "Careful," but when he came into the bedroom she was lying back on the bed in her clothes with her legs together and her hands at her sides.

He sat down on the bed and picked at one of her hands. She kept her eyes on the ceiling. When he lifted her hand and laid it in his lap, she closed them. He looked out the window for a moment and then put her hand back at her side and went around the bed. He climbed on and lay beside her with his head against her stomach. He could hear her heart beating quickly and for a moment was surprised. He listened more closely and suddenly was reminded of himself with his ear pressed to the door of the clock. He couldn't hear anything over her heart, but presently he felt a light punch against his cheek, and he lay back beside her and closed his eyes.

JANUARY 1900

The Reverend Price preached on against the recanters through the winter. The hair had closed entirely over his head now and grew down almost as far as his shoulders. "Our Samson," they began to call him. It was said that he shaved three or four times a day, and people swore they had seen him practicing sermons in his kitchen with a Bible in one hand and a razor, flourished, in the other.

At New Year he spoke to them of evolution. "Professor Darwin writes that men only became men after a million years. First we were fish and then fowl and then swine and so on and so forth through every kind of beast until men." He shook his head. "Vain fancy. Has not the great scholar Bishop Usher made a careful accounting of all the generations begat through the Scriptures and proven the earth to be not above five thousand years old? Time enough for the Lord, but not for all the professor's changes. For what is change to Him that is unchanging? What is time to Him that can reach out and turn it back as easily as you move the hands on a pocket watch? Men are men and there's an end on it. The Lord God made us in His image, as surely as He put slate in these mountains for you." He paused for a moment to stare fiercely out at them. "And yet if Professor Darwin were living with us in Bethany today, he might not have so far to go to prove his point that man is descended from apes." He meant the *Cynffonwyr*, the men with tails, and with that he began to distribute a handbill with a list of their names.

On another occasion he handed out placards saying, "*Nid oes bradwr yn y ty hwn* — There is no traitor here," for the men to place in their parlour windows. Thomas asked Catrin's permission and she shrugged.

"What do I care?" she said.

He had stopped her going to chapel in the seventh month. She didn't show much, but ever since he had seen her struggling to kneel he made her keep indoors as much as possible. Even so, he felt people were talking about him behind his back.

123's hands healed in time for him to help move the furniture out of people's houses. Most men could have done it themselves, but few of them could bear to. They let the big man do it and shared some of the money they got for the pieces. At first they sold to relatives or friends — farmers from the valley, mostly — but soon there was more furniture on offer than the farmers knew what to do with and people from town — fishermen, shopgirls, domestics — began to come on trips to see what they could pick up.

Thomas's uncle still brought him potatoes once a week, saying, "I expect you'd win them from me at billiards by and by," so he sold only selected items. He would have liked Catrin to help him, but she told him, "You earned the money, you choose." He couldn't at first. He looked at the chaise and it seemed brand-new. He looked at the dresser and he could remember what Catrin had been wearing the day they chose it. *It might have been yesterday*, he thought.

He began with the peacock firescreen, which ended up in a hotel in Llandudno, and then sold off the china piece by piece. Only when he had sold the gravy boat and the butter dish to two giggling friends who worked at a milliner's in Caernarfon and came home brandishing two shillings did Catrin tell him that he should have sold the set whole. He told himself he would sell all the china and that that should see them through the spring, but in the end he had to let the dresser go in February. He thought about selling the clock, but the thought that he'd not get six guineas, let alone twelve, for it stopped him. He couldn't bear to let it out of the house in its mutilated state. It would be admitting something he wasn't prepared to admit to himself or Catrin or the village.

The other thing 123 did when his hands healed was begin to harry the scabs. Old Cyril Morris had been one of the first to return. 123 had gotten into the habit of mooning around the Morris's house, ever since Mair had started stepping out with a farmer from the valley, but her father had usually been able to send him packing. Now, when the scab opened the door and told him to be off, 123 stood his ground. Cyril came halfway up the path and whispered, "I've Mair to think about," and 123 laughed in his face. "Hiding behind a girl!" But when Mair herself came out and asked him to leave them be, he turned on his heel. "Who else is going to do it, Roy?" she called to his back. "Support me and Mother?" It wasn't long after that he began visiting the homes of other scabs. His favourite trick was to tie the handles of their doors shut and then, alone or with others, walk around the house, booing.

Early on he tried to enlist Thomas in these nocturnal activities, but Catrin wouldn't hear of it. "His place is here of an evening," she told her brother. They were in the kitchen, Catrin standing behind Thomas where he sat by the fire. He had already begun to reach for his jacket, and now he started to protest. "Don't!" she told him. Her tone was angry, but the hands she pressed down on his shoulders were warm and he settled back into his chair. "And you," she said, wheeling on her brother, "don't think to be welcome here if I hear you speak of this again." The big man looked as if he wasn't sure whether to laugh or be angry, but before he could say anything, she stepped out from behind her husband's chair and stood with her hands on her hips, her weight on her heels, and her small, hard belly thrust forward like a clenched muscle. 123 met her gaze for a moment and then let his eyes fall.

"I see I'd best be going," he said, flushing.

Afterwards, Thomas told her she'd shamed him.

"Are you such a fool that you want to go?"

"It's the principle of the thing," he said. "Those fellers have no principles. They've no pride."

"They've wives and children, don't they? Isn't that enough?"

She stood over him where he sat and he kept his head bowed, staring at her belly. This was her ninth month, and the baby, by his reckoning, was already almost two weeks overdue, but she had said nothing. At night he lay awake figuring the dates, and when he finally fell into a fitful sleep, he dreamed she was holding it in, that the delivery might be postponed indefinitely, that she might go on being pregnant for months.

After that night, 123 didn't call again. Thomas still saw him about the streets, but he found other company in the evenings. The scabs put up with his antics, partly out of fear of what more he might do if they confronted him, partly out of fear of what the dragoons would do to him if they told. They ignored him as best they could and went about their lives as before. They even continued to attend services, slipping in late after everyone was seated and taking the furthermost pews, until one Sunday in February when the reverend, red in the face, his sideburns running with sweat, turned on them.

"There are, among the ranks of falterers and balkers, those who have been heard to say their God has failed them." He shook his head slowly. "Far better and more becoming these backsliders to have held their peace! For I say unto you, it is they who have failed their God, and this chapel. And no man who betrays his fellow workers can belong to Christ's religion."

There was a commotion at the back of the room. Dafydd and Arthur began to look round, but Thomas put his arms around them both.

"What are we fighting for?" shouted a voice. It might have been Cyril Morris. "Can you tell me that? Can someone please remind me?"

There was a long silence; even the reverend, shaking the hair from his eyes, seemed at a loss. Finally the tension was interrupted by a long drawn-out fart from the front of the chapel, and from where he sat, Thomas could see 123 Davies's shoulders shaking with laughter. The big man tipped his head back and put a large shell to his lips and blew again until the spittle flew.

There was the sound of running feet and then the door slamming and then the Reverend Price saying, "Without hope, is there not still determination? Without comfort, is there not still resolve?" He leaned forward over the lectern toward them. "Without work, are there not still men? I tell you, my people, we are fighting to win. You have been used, as you say, to winning the slate from the earth. Now you must win your very souls from your bodies. Each day fought is a day of victory. What we have begun we must carry forth. The standard we have lifted cannot be set down. For if only a hundred, if only ten, nay, if even one man alone carries it onward, we will have victory."

The reverend met them all at the door of the chapel on their way out. Thomas could see him shaking hands and speaking to the men before him.

"Kenneth," the reverend said, and clasped a hand in greeting. "Be a man. Douglas," he said to the next in line, "Be a man. Gwyn. Be a man, eh?"

Thomas pushed Dafydd and Arthur before him and held out his hand before the reverend even called his name.

"Thomas," the reverend said. "We haven't seen Catrin in chapel these few weeks. I hope nothing's amiss?"

The reverend's palms were rough with stubble, but he kept on shaking hands while Thomas said, "No, no. A little poorly, perhaps. Nothing to speak of."

"Be a man," the reverend said, nodding, and released him into the gray February day. "Hugh," he called to the next in line.

After that day the recanters began to apply to attend the Anglican church in the valley below. Soon they were the only villagers welcome in the valley. Farmers, Thomas's uncle among them, had lost a number of sheep in recent weeks, and although there was some foolish talk of a great hairy beast ravaging the flocks, the more sensible opinion was that it must be hungry strikers.

MARCH

The evening in March when Mr. Randall posted a notice of the remaining jobs at the quarry, Catrin's water broke. Thomas met 123 in the street and told him the news; the company would be taking back only three hundred of the nine hundred men who had worked before the strike.

"How can that be?" 123 said. In the bright spring sunlight, the ridge of his brows cast his eyes in deep shadow. "How can they say they don't need us?"

"They don't need as much slate, so they don't need as many men. They say that as soon as they have three hundred men the strike will be over."

"And who the bloody hell are they to say it's over? We're the ones is on strike."

Thomas shrugged.

"We'll see about this," the big man said. He began to stride off in the direction of the chapel, but turned once and called back in encouragement, "This changes nothing, mind." He grinned and shook a fist in the air. "The strike'll never end."

When Thomas got home he told Catrin that it was out of their hands now. She shook her head. She wanted to know how many men had already gone back.

"Perhaps a hundred," he said.

"And how many do you think will go back tomorrow?"

she said. He hung his head. Men had left the village to take up jobs in the coal fields of the south, even to emigrate, but he knew there were more than enough left for the remaining jobs. Catrin was waiting for him. She was so big now, so solid, that he felt insubstantial before her. "How many?"

"How should I know?" he snapped, and that was when her water broke. It poured out of her, covering the kitchen floor and lapping out the door.

"Jesus," he said, and left her there while he ran next door for Mrs. Lloyd.

Soon the house was full of women. They helped Catrin up to her bed and hustled Thomas and the boys — who had been playing in the street — out of the kitchen. Thomas tried to follow Mrs. Lloyd upstairs when she filled a basin with hot water, but she stopped on the first step and gave him such a look that he stayed where he was. He and the boys ended up sitting stiff-backed in the parlour, the only place where they were out of the way, listening to the scuff of feet above their heads.

Thomas passed out sheets of newspaper for the boys to put their wet feet on. When the cries started, he caught Arthur in his arms and pressed his hands over the boy's ears. The house was so small there was nowhere to go to escape the noise. Like that, though, he couldn't catch Dafydd before the boy slipped off his seat and bolted out the front door.

He kept his hands pressed over Arthur's ears, despite his squirming, until, finally exhausted, the boy fell asleep against him. He relaxed his grip but kept his hand under his son's head, feeling the warm dampness of his hair. He stared at the stuffed, rearing weasel under its glass until the cries ended. His eyes fell on the reverend's notice in the window and he read it to himself, spelling out the letters. Then he looked up at the clock. When he knew they would be coming down for him soon, he took first one hand and then the other from Arthur's ears, carried him to bed, and pulled the covers up to his chin. He went back into the parlour and stilled the clock for fear that the chimes would disturb the new baby.

He heard feet on the landing and then on the stairs.

"Mr. Jones?" It was Mrs. Lloyd, beckoning him. She was smiling broadly. He followed her up the stairs into the bedroom. Smiling women, too many for him to count, filed past him with murmured goodnights. Then he sat for a spell with his wife and new daughter.

Catrin held the baby to her chest, and he stroked first the child's face and then the mother's.

"Take her," Catrin said weakly, and he held the baby, cupping its smooth hairless head in his palm, until both mother and child fell asleep. When he heard sounds downstairs, he got up quickly and left them with the neighbour.

Dafydd was standing on one foot in the kitchen, the old bowler tipped forward rakishly as he pulled at his other boot. Thomas held a finger to his lips.

"Where've you been?" he whispered.

"With Uncle 123," the boy whispered back. "We went all over town. We tied their door handles and threw sods down their chimneys and when they opened the windows to let out the smoke we threw in dead rats." He giggled.

"Shh," Thomas said. "They can hear every word upstairs."

"123 says I can go with him every night," the boy said.

"Shh!" Thomas only meant to slap him lightly, but the blow sounded very loud in the quiet kitchen. The hat spun around on the kitchen floor, and the boy started crying.

"The reverend saw us," he said. "He thought it was funny."

"Shh," Thomas hissed and struck him again. "Shh!" When the boy was calm, he took him up to see his new sister.

Thomas slept in the parlour and dreamed of work. He was bent over a slate with his mallet resting on the head of his chisel, studying the slab. All around him men were working, striking their chisels to cleave the slate and then using them like levers to pry the stone apart with a swift tearing sound. The men were talking, too, all together and excitedly, but Thomas couldn't make out the words. He watched their lips move, but he couldn't hear them over the hammering. He woke to the sound of a hundred chisels tapping at slate and realized it was boots in the street. Standing at the window, blinking in the predawn light, he saw men coming down the street, a dozen or more, with 123 towering above them in the centre of the group.

Thomas felt a lightness in his stomach as he watched

them slowly approach. He bent down for his boots and stood on one leg to pull them on, never taking his eyes off the marching men. When they were close enough for him to see the grim set of their faces, he stepped into the hall. He stood behind the front door for a moment, breathing deeply, and then opened it and stepped out, pulling it shut behind him. He walked to the end of the path and stood by his gate in his shirtsleeves, waiting for them. He kept his eyes on 123, but the big man wouldn't look at him, and Thomas felt himself flush in the chill morning air.

As they came closer, he saw that 123 was carrying something, and as they passed him, without breaking stride, he saw that it was the reverend. 123 held him like a child, but his head rolled in the big man's arms and a long loop of thick black hair swung loosely almost to the ground.

People were coming out of their houses along the street, and Thomas became conscious, without really knowing who said it, that the reverend had fallen into the quarry. Thomas had seen men fall before. It took a long time and wasn't over until the frayed end of their safety rope fell about them in the shape of a snake or a noose.

Some people began to follow the body, but Thomas only watched them go. He heard someone say that a couple of sheep had fallen into the pit too, and he thought, *There'll be mutton today at the quarry*. The light was stronger now, flashing off the windows higher up the hill, and he stepped inside to get ready.

Before he left, he went up to see Catrin. She was pale

and drawn, but her eyes when she opened them were bright. The baby lay tiny and still against her breast.

"I'll have Mrs. Lloyd come by and sit with you," he whispered. "The boys are still asleep, at least."

He was dressed for work, and he saw her gaze drift up to the battered bowler hat on his head. He took it off and turned it in his hands.

"I've lost my pride," he told her with a weak smile.

She considered him for a moment, and he shifted his weight from foot to foot.

"I'm proud of you," she said.

He sat on the bed then and bowed his head, but she placed her hands around his face and lifted it. "It suits you," she said, and he tried to laugh. For a moment he thought she was going to kiss him, but then she reached up and settled the hat back on his head.

SAFE

BUTCH SHOULD HAVE KNOWN it would come to this when the Kid started shooting ostriches again.

They were sheltered under a small stand of trees just outside the town, the horses lying on the ground and the men across their necks. A light rain was falling, and it sounded to Butch like the crackling of fire as it pattered off the leaves above them. The Kid held out a bottle, but Butch shook his head. He hunkered down over his horse and waited for dusk to fall.

The ostriches had been his first plan when Ella had said the money was running out. "An ostrich ranch," he'd told them. "We'll sell the feathers to New York and Paris, the eggs here in town. Hell, I bet your ostrich even makes a fine roasting bird." They looked at him dubiously.

"You ever ate it?" the Kid asked.

"I've ate snake, ain't I?" Butch said. "I've ate possum and squirrel and raccoon."

"What's that got to do with ostrich?" Ella wanted to know.

"Cain't taste worse, can it? Cain't taste worse than snake."

The Kid nodded slowly.

"Nuthin' worse than snake."

"There you are!" Butch said. "Besides, the feathers is where we'll make the real money."

How had he been supposed to know that you couldn't herd ostriches? "Just tell me," he said to the Kid, "have you ever in your life seen a creature couldn't be herded?"

The first bird they saw stuck its head in the sand as soon as it spotted them riding toward it. Its strong, muscular neck twitched as they walked their horses around it, and it kept shifting its body to keep them always in the rear. Every so often it flicked out one of its long taloned claws in their direction and the horses skittered.

"That thing'll gut a horse with one kick," the Kid warned.

They circled it warily until Butch was on one side of the ostrich and the Kid on the other and it couldn't threaten them both.

"So," the Kid called. "What now?"

"Rope 'im, of course."

"Cain't get no rope over his head if it's stuck in the dirt."

Butch considered this. They'd set out for the plain before dawn, but now the sun was high overhead. He untied his kerchief and pressed it to the mouth of his canteen and wiped his face.

"Tricky little bastard," he said at length.

In the end, he threw a rope under the ostrich and the Kid threw it back to him over the bird. Butch tied a loop and tightened it until it closed on the ostrich's neck. He gave a tug, but the bird didn't move. He spurred his horse back and pulled tighter and the ostrich crumpled to the desert floor.

"Think ya broke his neck."

Butch tied the rope off on his pommel and climbed down.

"Must have been ailing already," he said.

" 'Spect so."

Butch stood over the body for a moment, shaking his head. Then he bent down, took hold of a handful of feathers, and began to pull. He braced his boot against the bird's rump and tried again.

"It's coming," he said, but instead he felt the whole bird rising under him. For a moment he thought he was pulling it and he pressed down harder with his boot, but the bird kept moving. Butch looked up and there was its head peering at him.

The way the Kid told it later, Butch took off back to his horse and the bird upped and chased him. "It'd have got him, too, if I hadn't hit it a couple of times." The Kid's first two shots hit the bird in the rump, and it almost fell. Instead, it stopped to get its balance and turned toward him. By the time it charged, shrieking and flapping its tiny wings, Butch was back in the saddle to see the Kid make the shot. It was a beauty. From the back of a bucking horse, he blew the bird's head off from fifteen feet.

"Shit," Butch said.

They used their knives to cut a bunch of feathers free and presented them in a bouquet to Ella. She stuck them in her hair, and in the buttonholes of her dress, and they took turns dancing with her, their feet dragging over the boards. They told her that they didn't think ostrich ranching was for them.

The rain was getting heavier, but at least it was dark now. Butch let the horse up and tethered it to a stake he'd brought for the purpose. He watched the glow of the oil lamp in the back of the little bank, while beside him the Kid pulled his slicker around him, trying to keep his guns dry.

They'd promised Ella on the boat to put her in charge of the money when they finally settled, and in return she'd demanded that they put it in a bank. The Kid had been downright offended about that and Butch himself had called it unnatural, but she had insisted. She opened the account in her name, too, because, as she said, "The Kid cain't read or write so he's got no part in business and I'm not opening an account with Butch and set people's tongues wagging." The Kid was an easygoing fella, and Ella was liberal with her favors — Butch had no complaints — but in public she insisted she was with the Kid. It was always his arm she took if they ever went into town, and on the narrow boardwalks Butch would have to skulk along behind. He had tried to tell them the Kid should have both hands free, just in case, but they wouldn't listen.

"Anyway," Ella had said when she'd told them about the bank, "if you want the money badly enough, you can always make a withdrawal."

As a concession she let them choose where they wanted to settle, and they had travelled for weeks from town to town, with the boys sizing up banks that looked safe enough to trust their money to. Butch still had a list in his head of those that didn't. In the end, they had come to Patagonia because of the Welsh.

"They're good with money," the Kid had said when Butch told him about the community of Welshmen.

"That's the Scots," Butch had told him.

"What's the difference?" the Kid had asked, and Butch had had to admit he didn't know.

"Well then," the Kid said. "At least they're white and they speak English."

The Kid had been horrified when it turned out that the Welshmen spoke Welsh. He'd been under the impression that all white men spoke one language. The explosive glottal sounds of Welsh had set his gun hand twitching and he'd been all for heading out of town.

Butch, however, was tired and insisted on having a look in the bank. While Ella had tried to make herself understood by the one teller, he had stared hard at the big green safe just visible in the back office. When she had lost patience and tried to pull him away, he had hauled her back to the teller. "Good morning," he said. "I'd like to see the manager." The young fellow behind the counter shrugged and opened his hands.

"Come on," Ella said. "We're wasting our time."

Butch took the small carpetbag from her hand. He set it on the counter and opened it and took out a bundle of notes, and then another and another. The teller squirmed off his stool in a moment and returned with a stocky older man with curly black hair. The manager put a hand on Butch's arm and opened a small gate in the counter. Butch stepped back to let Ella and the Kid go first and then swept the money back into the bag. He tipped his hat to the teller.

In his office, the manager held out his hand.

"Robert Evans," he said.

"Smith," said Butch.

"Jones," said the Kid.

"Mrs. Jones," said Ella.

"Ah," the manager said. "A good Welsh name. I must apologize for not speaking to you in English before, but the community was founded upon the principle of preserving our language. The use of English is frowned upon even for those that know it."

"But not by you," Butch said.

"I'm a businessman," Evans said. "English is the language of business." He smiled, and Butch met his eye and smiled back.

"Tell me about your safe," Butch said. "I don't know the maker."

Evans had brought the safe from Wales himself, he said. He'd been a clerk in a bank in Liverpool when he had heard about the colony in Patagonia, and he had spent all his savings and a small inheritance from his mother to book passage and to buy the safe. "South Walian steel, is that, gentlemen," he said, slapping it resoundingly. He had arrived on the beach of a new continent with the safe and nothing else. Inside it on the passage he had kept a bedroll, a change of clothes, a photograph of his mother, and a letter of reference from the chief teller at his bank in Liverpool. He pointed to the letter framed above his head. On the beach, he had built a sled for the safe and hauled it inland himself. He'd not been able to keep up with the other settlers, and they warned him about savages, but he'd told them that if he saw signs of trouble he would climb inside the safe. It took him two weeks to reach the town. He dragged the safe within sight of the church, judged it "near enough my God to thee," and afterwards never moved it an inch. He built the bank around it. For weeks he traded out of the safe itself, sitting with his back to it with an umbrella over his head. When he finally finished the bank, he'd built it with a bedroom and a kitchen at the back for himself to live in.

The way he talked about it, Butch could believe the tough little man had mined the ore and smelted the metal to make the safe himself. He liked him, and he told the Kid the bank was as safe as any he'd seen in South America, which was true, although it didn't mean much.

Butch had been trying to come up with another plan ever since the ostriches. The problem was that they were supposed to be going straight in South America, and it limited his thinking. Not that Butch wanted to go back to thieving — he was getting too old for all the riding — but he thought that the Kid wanted to. When the Kid went off every few days to shoot ostriches and bring back more feathers for Ella, Butch knew that really he was practising, getting his eye back in.

Going straight had been their idea, Butch and Ella's together. He'd liked it when they'd both been on the same side, trying to persuade the Kid.

It wasn't that Butch didn't have ideas; he had plenty, but he couldn't settle on a good one. They could go gold panning in the Andes. Evans had told him the Andes would be as big as the Klondike. All it needed, the banker said, was a few good men to go up to the hills and get the gold rush started. "Just think," he said dreamily. "With enough gold coming through here, I could afford a brick vault and steel bars on the windows."

"That's some ambition," Butch had told him.

There was Indian hunting, too. The Argentine government offered cash for the head or balls of any Indian, but Butch didn't want to mention it to the Kid in case he liked the idea too much. Butch didn't mind saying he was scared of Indians, and besides, the Kid was only fair with a rifle, although he'd never admit it, and most of that work would be done with a rifle.

Then there was the dinosaur. The Smithsonian museum in Washington, no less, had a standing offer of $10,000 for a whole dinosaur skeleton, and Butch had heard of a place over the desert where you just had to dig and you'd find bones galore. Butch liked the sound of that, but he knew the Kid would never go for it. He didn't turn a hair at fresh death, but he was oddly skittish around boneyards.

Butch knew he couldn't afford another plan like the ostrich ranch. He was sure the Kid had told Ella everything in bed. That would be why Ella was saying now that they should just buy some cattle and start a real ranch. Butch didn't fancy that. He'd been a cowboy when he was younger and that was why he'd turned to thieving in the first place. It had been hard work when he was a boy. He didn't think he could take it any better now.

What worried him more was that Ella should be suggesting anything. That was his job. They had agreed that she should be in charge of the money, but it had always been Butch who worked out how they'd make more. That's how it had always been with the Kid and him, and he expected Ella to go along. He had to come up with a good plan to keep Ella in line, and he had to come up with a good plan or the Kid might just leave.

Butch didn't want to think about that. He'd become so reliant on the Kid's gun that he couldn't imagine being safe without him. Even a goddamned ostrich might have got him if the Kid hadn't been around. Even going straight there were still enough fellas out there who might come looking for him. Some Pinkertons had been asking questions in town, but they'd all been referred to Evans at the bank, because of his English, and he hadn't given them the time of day.

"They were looking for Americans," the little Welshman said. "So I knew it couldn't be you or Mr. Jones."

Butch liked the Welshman — even told him to call him Butch — but it made him think that he used to like the Kid more. Back at Hole-in-the-Wall, he was sure he had. But then the Kid had been part of the gang, and now they were partners and things were different.

If the Kid left, he thought, Ella might go with him.

"I could be a gunfighter," the Kid had said a week after the ostrich.

Butch had looked hard at him.

"You know, a hired gun. Sure."

"You sack of shit," Butch said. "You couldn't get hired to jerk off."

The Kid was on his feet with his gun out.

"Sorry, Kid," Butch mumbled. He took another mouthful of coffee. "Didn't mean anything by it."

The Kid holstered his gun after a moment and sat down.

"But you see," Butch said. "It'd have been murder. Gunslinger's got to make the other guy reach first. Make it self-defence. You're too fast, Kid. No one wants to draw on you. You gotta make 'em."

The Kid was silent. Then he said, "You son of a bitch. You bastard. You . . ." He paused. "You son of a bitch!"

"Sorry, Kid," Butch said. He sipped his coffee.

"Shit." The Kid got to his feet and ran out the door. On the porch, Butch heard him stalk back and forth, muttering, "Son of a bitch." The Kid had taken it out on the ostriches the next day, and Butch had felt oddly guilty for the carnage.

In the end, he told them about the Andes. He tried to make it sound good, but he could tell he was losing them.

"How long do you think it'll take to make it up there?" Ella said.

"A year," Butch said. "Two at the most. It'll be hard,

but after that we'll be able to retire for good. We'll live like kings."

The Kid and Ella looked at each other.

"What?" Butch said.

"We can't — " the Kid began, but Butch cut him off.

"You don't know what you're talking about. I've looked into this."

"Ella's pregnant," the Kid said.

Butch didn't know what to say. He felt like going for his gun.

"Is it time?" the Kid said. Butch looked at his watch and it was. He felt nervous for the first time in years. At least the rain had stopped. The Kid was loading dry shells.

"It'll be easy," Butch told him. "Don't go shooting anyone unnecessary."

They swung up into the saddle and walked the horses toward the light. The Kid's began to whinny and he had to talk to her quietly. His best horse was with Ella on the edge of the desert. She'd be there now, Butch thought, waiting for them. He wondered what would happen if only one of them met her and if she had a choice which one she'd prefer.

She'd kissed them both when they rode off, but she'd been with the Kid the night before. At one point she'd come out to find Butch smoking in the rocker. "Get some sleep," she'd said quietly. "We'll be together tomorrow night."

He'd sat and smoked and she'd gone outside to the privy. When she walked back she stopped beside him and put a hand on the back of the rocker to still him. He could smell her hair as she stooped over and put her lips to his ear.

"It could be yours," she said.

He didn't say a word, didn't even breathe until she straightened up and went back inside and he went back to his rocking. He found his cigarette had gone out.

There was no whorehouse for twenty miles — the Welsh wouldn't have one in their town — and Butch had taken to drinking with Evans on nights when he wasn't wanted. He told the Welshman that Mr. and Mrs. Jones needed their privacy. Besides, Evans was the only one in town who'd speak English to him.

He'd asked him once to come to the whorehouse with him, but the Welshman had shaken his head sadly.

"Not for me," he said. "I tried a sporting girl once. In Liverpool." He shuddered. "No thanks."

"Well, what do you do?" Butch said. He'd had a few drinks by then.

"I wait for some homely little settler-girl to get off the boat." He saw the look on Butch's face. "You could too. All you'd need to do is learn a little Welsh. The girls won't mind if you don't say much. I could teach you."

"How can you wait?"

"Butch, *bach*," the Welshman said expansively. "We're part of history here. Our children will be speaking Welsh in a hundred years. Even after they stop speaking it at home. Even after they stop being Welsh in Wales. Look at me. I was a nobody in Liverpool. Now . . ." He gestured to the bank around them. "You've got to take the long view."

He poured Butch another drink.

"D'you know," he said, "the first Welshman to set foot in these parts was a pilot for Darwin."

Butch would have liked to go and see Evans last night, but of course it had been impossible.

They tied the horses with slipknots to the rail outside the bank, and Butch knocked. He knocked quietly, but he kept it up for a long time, and eventually they heard movement and a voice behind the door.

"Who is it?"

"It's Smith."

Evans opened the door and welcomed them inside. He was in the middle of his supper and he still had a big square napkin tucked into his collar, hanging down over his stomach. He looked a little comic, but Butch liked him for it.

"Come for a bit of peace and quiet, eh?" he said, and then he saw the Kid.

"Ella's pregnant," Butch said. "Mrs. Jones," he added when he saw the Welshman's confusion.

"Oh, aye? That's grand. Congratulations." He held out his hand to the Kid.

It was all over very quickly once they were inside. The Kid pulled his gun and Evans opened the safe. He refused at first.

"You know this is my bank," he said to Butch. "I'm not part of a big company. If you rob me, I'll be ruined. Why should I help you? Kill me. I'm ruined anyway."

Butch showed him the dynamite.

"You can still have the safe," he said gently. "You can take it someplace else and start again."

He'd got on his knees and opened it for them then,

but afterwards, when they were stuffing the money — not much, Butch thought — into the saddlebags, Evans said, "I'm too old to go dragging a safe around the country anymore."

"Go prospecting," Butch said. "The Andes. You can sell the safe and buy grub and a mule and pans and everything you need. Sure." He thought if he could persuade Evans, the idea wouldn't be entirely wasted.

"No," the Welshman said. "I'm a banker. I've always worked in a bank."

"Like us," the Kid said. "We've always been robbers."

He smiled, and Evans smiled back at him as if they were old friends and took a step toward him.

"No," Butch said. He was talking to Evans, but it was the Kid who turned toward him. Butch could have gone for his gun, but he didn't. He stood and watched. The Kid wasn't a big fella, and once the Welshman was on him he was always going to be stronger. He twisted the Kid's gun out of his hand and turned it on him.

"Now, boys," he began, but the Kid was going for the gun he kept in his belt. Evans pulled the trigger, but nothing happened. He tried again, but by then the Kid had his second gun out. He fanned the hammer once and Evans fell back. The napkin, still fixed at his neck, settled softly over his chest, and a stain began to spread across it.

The Kid picked up the gun he'd dropped. He shook it in the Welshman's face.

"No trigger," he said. "I wired it back. It's faster to fan."

He turned and moved to the door and stopped beside Butch.

"Where were you?" he said.

"I'm getting too old for this." Butch stood a moment more. He was still holding the gun he had belatedly drawn, although the Kid had already holstered his and had the saddlebags in his hands.

"It's all right," the Kid said. "He's dead."

Butch wondered what it would be like riding out to Ella alone. He could see her in the distance, the way she sat a horse, with her back very straight. She'd be wearing the hat he bought her in New York City, with her hair jammed up under it, exposing her neck. But when he imagined her face seeing him alone, he closed his eyes. He twirled his gun and dropped it into the holster.

"Hey," the Kid said. "Fancy."

I DON'T KNOW WHAT DO YOU THINK?

THERE ARE WAYS you can tell if someone is serious about killing themselves. You can never be sure and you should always assume they mean what they say, but there are ways. Things like: Has anyone in their family or anyone they've ever known committed suicide?

What stops most people is the thought of what it would do to those they leave behind. Even at our lowest point we think of other people's feelings. I've talked to people who couldn't bring themselves to do it because they couldn't bear to have someone find them. Even a stranger. One woman told me she felt like she would be imposing. She realized the milkman would find her, and because she opened the door to him at Christmas and gave him some money and he told her about his kids, she couldn't.

On the other hand, if a person knows someone who has killed themselves, it changes the way they look at it. That's the first sign.

* * *

My name is Clive and I joined Lifeline in 1988. We get a lot of different calls, but unlike other help lines we're specifically set up for suicides.

What made me join, and it surprised me, was something the fellow said at the recruitment meeting. I hadn't even gone along to join. All I'd heard was that they were short of money, and I thought I might be able to help with fund-raising. I used to do that at Carol's school when they were collecting for the new gym, and I wanted to show that I could still be useful after the layoff. Anyway, what this fellow said was that Lifeline's policy was not to dissuade people. If someone called him up and told him they'd just swallowed a bottle of pills and wanted someone to talk to while they died, he said he'd do it. He wouldn't try to trick them into saying where they were, even though it would be easy when they got drowsy. He would respect that person's right to die. I found that impressive, that attitude to death. I don't even know if I agreed with it, but I looked at him saying it and I thought, *I've got to find out more about this.*

Don't expect to join Lifeline to feel good, I remember them saying in training. Don't do it to feel heroic. The object of the exercise is to make the other person feel good. How you feel is irrelevant. You can't know if you've done any good. You'll never know what happens to them after they hang up. All you can do is listen to them for as long as they want to talk to you.

That made me think. I used to work for the phone company. I installed the exchange for this town back in the fifties when it was all electromechanical, before they tore everything out and installed the new system. The point is, I thought I knew about telephones. The idea of someone you've never met, someone you'll never meet, calling you up from out of the blue — the possibility of that — made me look at phones differently. Anyone can call you up and say anything and you'll never ever be able to talk to them again once they hang up. That's your whole contact with them. It's like a call from Mars.

I never expected Lifeline would want me, of course. I was fifty-three then and I thought they would want someone younger. But no, they said they didn't have enough fellows my age, so I signed up for the training. Carol, I'm pretty sure, would have approved — she was always volunteering for things when she was at college — but my wife, Helen, looked doubtful. No more than me, really. She didn't think that ordinary people did those sorts of things. She thought you needed to be some kind of saint or reformed drug addict and I think she thought I was putting on airs thinking I could give people advice just because we had had our loss. I told her that had nothing to do with it and I was shocked that she thought that. "I could understand your acting funny if Carol killed herself," I said. And she said, "Don't talk stupid."

Now she tells all her friends that I'm just doing it to meet people.

The thing that Helen doesn't understand is that you don't give advice. Of course, you could, you want to, but your advice wouldn't necessarily help. You can't hope to understand what the other person's going through and you should never say that you do. *They* probably don't understand what they're going through.

How could you? It's like saying, "Everyone feels like that sometimes." That only makes them feel stupid for calling you, as if their problem is nothing. It's just common sense.

Helen doesn't even talk to me about it anymore. She thinks she shouldn't because it's all confidential, and she's right, but I think I would tell her if she asked me. I used to tell her all about my training. She could have come along to some of the open sessions. They used to bring in the most remarkable people to break down our prejudices. That's where I met Mary.

Mary was a transsexual who they invited to come and talk to us. Helen was appalled by that. She didn't think there were any in our town. I suppose she thought they were all in London. The first thing that struck me about Mary was that she was about my age. When she was a man she — he? — used to be an architect. She said she had always wanted to be a woman, which is where I generally part company with these people. I just don't see how you could want something when you never had it. But then one thing she said did really impress me. She said that after the various operations she went back to her company and tried to get her old job back. And this was in this city, mind you. They took her back, too, but they wanted her to be a secretary. That made me laugh, which was embarrassing, but afterwards I went up to her and explained that it reminded me of myself trying to get a new job and that's why I laughed. Everywhere I went they kept telling me I was overqualified and then offering me clerical work. Mary said, "I remember when they used to say you could be out of a job in this town on a Friday night —"

"— and back in one on Monday morning," I said. I remembered those days.

Of course, the calls I take now are just as interesting as the training and sometimes I really would like to hear what Helen thinks. I can't see the harm, because she'll never know who the people are any more than I do. The whole thing about confidentiality is a bit misunderstood. Lifeline leaves it like that deliberately. They say the service is confidential, but they encourage us to talk about our calls with each other. To share it if we need to. It makes sense. I think of it like a chain down which some terrible hurt is passed. It starts out with the caller, who passes on a share of it to you, and then you pass it out in smaller and smaller shares to all the other people until it becomes bearable. Talking does that.

I met Mary again in the queue for the dole a few weeks after I started taking calls. I asked her if she'd like a coffee, but she said she'd love a pint. She said that she felt fine going into a coffee shop alone, but she didn't think it was right for her to go into a pub by herself and she didn't have many friends to go with. After she had a couple, she told me she knew it was unladylike, but she did miss the beer. Helen doesn't drink, herself, and I've lost touch with most of the lads from the office, so we make quite good drinking partners and now we meet once a week after I finish a stint on the phones. It's a little strange, I have to admit. The first time I saw

Mary I didn't think, There's a bloke in a dress. I just thought she was a big woman. Somebody said that to her at the meeting.

"What were you?" they said. "Six foot, six-one, when you were a man?"

And she said, "I've lost a few inches, love, but not in height."

Anyway, I don't feel embarrassed being out with Mary. I just find myself staring at her sometimes to see what she might have looked like as a man. I can't imagine it. Sometimes I even look at myself in the mirror and try and imagine my face as a woman's, but then all I see is Carol.

Another thing Mary misses is the football, and I've offered to go to a game with her whenever she wants, but she says she's still a little nervous. "I lose control at football," she says. "When United got to the Cup final, I fell to my knees on the terraces. I was in tears. Everybody was hugging everyone else." I like football, but I've never felt like that. I asked her how she could take it so seriously and she said, "I suppose I've always been an emotional person. I couldn't care about the big things if I didn't care about the little things too." I asked her if she didn't miss being a man, and she said, "Only the beer and the football."

Her name used to be Martin and she was originally from Yorkshire, although she doesn't have much of an accent. She has one sister still in the north, but they haven't been in touch for years. She says it's like having the memories of another person. "Martin's dead and buried," she says. "Did himself in. Good riddance."

Legally, she can't get her name changed on her birth certificate, which makes her angry, although it seems like sense to me. Once when she'd had a few pints, she said she only kept the pictures of Martin as a little boy and sometimes she felt like his mother. She laughed and laughed, but she's been more careful about how much she drinks now. The hormones have lowered her tolerance, she says, and whenever I try and buy her another one she waves me away: "No thanks. The hormones, you know."

I used to think that I could really help someone if they were depressed because they'd had a bereavement, but really I can't help them any more than I can help someone who rings up thinking they might have AIDS. My experience doesn't matter. I can't tell them what to do even if they ask me. People do call for advice, all the time, but we're taught not to give it. It's called reflecting the question. It's harder than it sounds. When we were training, the group leader sat us down in a circle and went round firing questions at people. All kinds of questions. "I'm pregnant. What should I do? I think I might be gay. What should I do? Who do you think's going to win the league this year?" To which you're supposed to answer, "I don't know. Who do you think's going to win it?" Anyhow, he asked me, "What do you think of Margaret Thatcher?" and I said, "Margaret Thatcher? Don't get me started."

That took me a long time to get the hang of. It just sounds so insincere, as if you're avoiding the question. Either that or it sounds like a riddle when you say, "I don't know," as if you're waiting for a punchline. The thing is, though, that callers don't want to hear about you, about your opinions or your troubles. They've got troubles of their own. They don't even want to hear your nerves. They're nervous enough. They don't want to have to take you into account as well.

Helen says she'd never ring a service like Lifeline. I used to agree with her, but now I think I probably would if I ever needed to. People think they should sort themselves out and they feel embarrassed about calling us, but really all we do is help them sort themselves out. I'd consider calling, certainly, but I suppose I've learned so much from the training and helping other people that I don't need to. I just think of the last person I talked to and I know my problems aren't so bad. Then Helen says she might have to ring just to talk to me one time. She's exaggerating. I only work three nights a week, and she gets enough of me under her feet all day as it is. I tell her she shouldn't joke about it. If she ever did call, she says, she'd ask for a female counsellor, and I tell her that's her privilege.

Mary says she only rang us once. She called from her hospital bed just before the final operation. She says she knew she was doing the right thing. She just wanted to talk to someone before they put her under. "Martin's last words," she says and pulls a face.

Mary used to ask me about Helen all the time and I told her a little about us and Carol, because it seemed only fair after everything she told me. She asked to see a photograph of Carol, which struck me as odd. I almost wanted to say, "Well, let's see a photograph of Martin," but I said I'd bring one with me next week and she was surprised that I didn't have one in my wallet. When she saw it she began to cry. I tried to take it from her, but she wouldn't let go and she kept saying, "How beautiful, how beautiful." It crossed my mind that it was the hormones again, but nothing would make her stop and people in the pub were beginning to look. I had to put my arm around her in the end and she pulled herself together.

"I never had children," she explained. "Of course, I can't have them now. The doctors are good — God bless 'em — but not that good."

After that, she began to say that she'd like to meet Helen, which seemed even odder to me. I had to be careful seeing Mary as it was. It would be pretty hard to explain if Helen ever found out. In the end, I told Mary that Helen would be jealous, which made her beam, although she knew only too well that many people had a bad reaction to her operation.

Consolation is a curious thing. A woman called me up and told me her name. "You've probably heard of my case," she said. "There's no point being coy." She was right. I had seen it in the newspapers. Her little girl had been missing and they had found her in a wood a month later. The woman said they'd buried her that morning, which I knew because Helen and I had seen the funeral on the news before I went out. I asked her how she was feeling and she said, "All right. Better than I have for a long time." She said that an old woman had come up to her as she was leaving the cemetery.

"You don't know me," the old woman said, "but I

know you. People will tell you you'll get over it. I lost my boy twenty years ago. You'll never get over it."

I asked the woman on the phone how that made her feel and she said, "Euphoric. It was the most consoling thing anyone has ever said to me." She thought it might be wrong to say that, but she didn't really care. Her husband didn't understand, she said. She just had to share it with someone.

I did get a call once from a father who'd lost his daughter. When he told me I felt this panic. I thought about getting his name and meeting him. I had this mad idea that we could be friends. I was lucky I'd been taking calls for a while by then. I kept everything professional and I think I helped him. It can never really be the same, I thought later. Carol was killed two years ago now. She was standing on a corner and a lorry took the turn too sharply and toppled over onto her. This man said his daughter had died of cancer. He sat by her bedside for three months. He called us because he said he couldn't mourn her properly. He said he forgot her for long stretches at a time and he would have to stop himself because he knew there was some reason to feel sad. "Am I a bad father, do you think?" he said. "I don't know," I said gently. "What do you think?" I thought that perhaps he had been mourning her all along while she was dying, but I couldn't tell him that.

I don't know if she planned it, but in the end Mary did manage to meet Helen. We were out in town one Saturday and I heard someone calling my name. It was

Mary. She told Helen that we knew each other from the office and then she said how much she liked Helen's hat. She was just going for a cup of tea and she asked why didn't we join her. I said I had to get back to the car because it was on a meter, thinking that Helen would come along, but she said she hadn't finished her shopping and Mary took her arm and they told me they'd meet me at a cafe. By the time I got there, they were already the best of friends. It hurt me because they were talking about Carol and I said, "This is ancient history," but Helen said softly, "Did you know that Mary lost her own son?"

"No," I said. "You never told me that."

"You just have to cut yourself off," Mary said. "It sounds awful, but you have to. It's the only way."

"Oh yes," said Helen, and her eyes were bright.

I didn't think I'd ever see Mary again after that, but Helen kept on and on about her. I almost told her the truth about Mary, but I couldn't do it. It annoyed me that Mary was deceiving my wife, especially as I knew Mary would be pleased about it, but I couldn't say anything. Helen just wouldn't stop talking about her. In the end, she called and invited Mary to dinner. I talked to her too, and she asked me if it was all right if she accepted and I didn't have the heart to say no. Then Helen took the phone back and said, "Oh, and bring your husband, of course."

Mary arrived with this bald, stocky fellow, Brian. I talked to him nearly all night, because as soon as they arrived Mary ran into the kitchen to be with Helen. I wasn't sure how much Brian knew, and he might not have been sure of me either, because all we talked about was football. He thought United should sell their old stars and invest in their youngsters, but I said I liked the old players. They weren't much good, but I knew them. "They're a bunch of has-beens," Brian said. "It's about time they let them go." Even after dinner, Mary said that she and Helen had important things to discuss and that she was going to help with the washing up. I listened to Brian drone on — he must have gone through the failings of every player on the team — but all my attention was fixed on the low murmur from the other room.

In bed, I asked Helen what Mary had said, and she told me, "Oh, she just wanted to explain about Brian. He's just a friend. Her husband ran off. Can you believe it? She didn't say, but I think it was around the time that her son died. Isn't that terrible? At least we have each other. We should be grateful for that."

I reached out and found her hand under the bedclothes and held it for a minute.

"She told me she thought we were a lovely couple," Helen said. Even in the darkness, I could tell from her voice she was smiling.

The worst calls, the ones we used to really dread when we were in training, are the silent calls. Worse than suicides. Worse than hoaxes. Hoaxes, by the way, you just have to ignore. You can never tell if it's a hoax or not. I got a call in my first week from a boy who said, "I like it when my girlfriend puts her finger up my arse. Do you think I'm bisexual?" I thought it might be a hoax but you can never tell. Usually, if you treat them seriously and they're a hoaxer they'll get embarrassed eventually. That's what they teach us, but this boy got embarrassed and I think that's understandable.

I got a silent call in my first week. A woman. I had her on the line for forty-five minutes and all she did was sob and say how sorry she was and all I did was keep telling her I was still there and that she should take her time and calm down and tell me what the trouble was. She sobbed for forty-five minutes. Right in my ear. A total stranger. I could hear her breathing. I could hear the clock ticking behind her. And she never told me what was wrong. She just hung up. Everyone was very concerned, but really I felt fine. It was just an incredible experience. I think I was almost in awe. In awe of the telephone. In awe of her suffering.

I actually haven't had too many suicides, and none that I think have gone through with it. I've had a lot of calls from people who are just depressed about life and their jobs, money problems, and I feel comfortable with these. Calls about relationships I think are harder. Not that the caller knows it. I just feel less optimistic. You dread the suicides at first and then you begin to want one, which I suppose is a terrible thing. It's like soldiers, I imagine — professional soldiers, not like us doing our national service. You train for something and it never happens. You want to find out if you can take it. I suppose the readiness is what counts.

I started to go to the football more regularly with Brian and Mary. United started the season pretty well for them, but by January they were beginning their traditional slide down the table.

"Pretty soon they'll be the strongest team in the league," Brian would say every time they lost. He meant they'd be at the bottom of the table, propping up the rest.

Football was really the only time I saw Mary anymore, and not to talk to properly. She kept telling me I should bring Helen down to a game. "We can all step out together," she said. "You and Helen and Brian and me." She put her arm through his. "We'd make quite an outing of it." She still called Helen quite often, but usually while I was at Lifeline. I missed our talks and felt a little jealous, but really I thought this was the way it should be.

One evening Helen asked me what I thought of Brian and I told her he seemed all right.

"Why?" I said.

"Mary asked me."

"And what did you say?"

"I told her I thought they made a lovely couple."

I had to stop myself smiling, but Helen must have seen something in my face, because she said, "What would a man know about it? She likes him, I tell you. You should have seen her light up when I told her. She was that happy."

Afterwards, I thought Helen must be wrong. Apart from anything else, I couldn't understand what Mary could see in Brian. He was such a know-it-all when it came to football.

Then one Saturday Brian turned up at the match

without Mary, and when I asked how she was, he said he didn't know. The way he said it made me say, "Oh?" And he said, "I never want to see that person again in my life. Don't ever ask me about them again."

When I got home I tried to call Mary. I planned to say I was just calling to tell her about the match and see if she wanted to talk. I left the game early anyway, so as not to get stuck in the car park. United were getting stuffed, although Brian stayed on, screaming abuse at the players. I don't think I could have dragged him away.

No one answered the phone at Mary's and I tried again and again. I told Helen that I thought Mary and Brian had had a row, but I didn't say about what. She came and sat by me as I rang. She said, "Put your hat and gloves on and go round if you want. But she won't thank you." I knew where Mary lived, but she'd never invited me in. "Martin always was an untidy bugger," she said. She was afraid something in her house would give her away.

"Sometimes people need to be alone. They're probably making up right now," Helen said. I think my ringing and ringing had begun to annoy her. "It's not your job," she said. "If she needs to talk, she knows our number." I looked at her and she said, "She's my friend too."

In the end, just before midnight, I got through.

"Mary? It's Clive," I said.

She asked me what I was doing calling so late, and by then it was too late to talk about football.

"We were just concerned about you," I said.

"I'm fine," she said, although I could hear she had been crying.

"We could come over," I offered, but she said, "No. It's not necessary."

I asked her if she was sure and she said she was very sure.

"Look after yourself," I said. She was silent for a moment. I could hear her pouring a drink, the bottle against the glass, the glass against her teeth. Her swallow.

"And you, Clive," she said. And she hung up.

For some reason, I kept the receiver to my ear. If you make the call, even if the other person puts the phone down they can't break contact. You're still there if they pick up the phone. For a moment I was sure Mary would come back on the line. *Now she'll pick up*, I thought. *Now*. But nothing happened, and the tension became so unbearable I hung up. I shouldn't stick my nose in where it wasn't wanted, I thought.

The next evening I looked in the paper and there was an announcement of death for a Martin K. I suppose I must have been looking for it. The street given was Mary's. I didn't tell Helen. I'm sure Mary wouldn't have wanted me to.

I just said the paper didn't come that night, and when Helen found me weeping, I said it was for Carol and she held me and said, "At last."

One last thing about confidentiality. I don't want to give anyone the wrong idea. I felt a bit funny the first time I told someone about a call, but now I know it has to be this way. Once, a young fellow rang me up and said he was frightened that his girlfriend was suicidal. He said she had been suicidal before he met her, and he thought that he could help, but now he no longer believed that. She was dragging him down and he wanted to leave her. "Is it terrible to want to leave her?" he asked me, and I had to say, "I don't know. What do you think?" And he said yes, he thought it was. He wasn't sure she wouldn't hurt herself, but he thought it was him or her now. He felt it was just survival now. The problem was he had no one to talk to about this. He thought it was disloyal to his girlfriend to say these things. That's what really convinced me that we have the right idea about talking to each other. I shouldn't have, but I told the boy some of the other ways to tell if someone is serious about suicide.

If they've put their affairs in order, that's another sign of seriousness. If they've made a will, or given things away, or settled old scores, those are all signs.

If they've thought of how they'd do it. Not just speculated about whether pills are better than gassing themselves in the garage, but thought about how many pills and which ones to take. If they've bought things to do it with, that's also a sign.

If they've tried before, it may or may not be a sign, I told him.

He told me it helped him. "You can only do so much," he said, "and then you have to let go for yourself. You can't look after them all their lives."

Of course, I never found out what actually happened to him or the girl.

COVENTRY

FRANK AND I are waiting for Lady Godiva. It's five to twelve and we're sat on a bench in Broadgate opposite the big clock waiting for the pubs to open. We've just been down to sign on and we need a pint.

"Come on," Frank says, his eyes on the clock. "Shake a leg, darling."

A group of old-age pensioners on a tour have begun to gather in front of us. Their guide, Lisa, is telling them all about Lady Godiva and her husband, Lord Leofric: how she rode naked through the streets of Coventry to protest his unfair taxes and how the peasants, when they heard what she was doing for them, ran indoors and pulled their shutters and sat in the dark until they heard her horse go by. "The original poll-tax demonstrator," Lisa calls her, and the OAPs chuckle and repeat the line to each other. Lisa is seventeen, but dressed older in a two-piece blue suit that makes her seem more skinny and angular than when we sleep together on her days off. She wears a light blue sash with the tourist board logo. It flaps against her chest in the wind.

"Wouldn't mind a cushy job like that, eh?" Frank says, a little too loudly.

"You'd look like bleeding Miss World," I tell him.

The clock strikes at last, and for a moment even the few shoppers hurrying for their buses stop and look up. The doors in the clockface slide open and Lady Godiva rides out onto the narrow balcony. She's painted bright pink apart from the yellow hair that falls over her shoulders. One thick rope of it runs down her back and spreads like a cape over the horse; the other falls like a sheet into her lap. She gets about halfway around when another door opens above her and a huge leering face, almost as big as Godiva herself, leans forward. It's Peeping Tom. He stares out for a moment, covers his face with his hands, and is drawn back into the darkness.

The OAPs ooh and aah and Frank complains for the umpteenth time that it's not very realistic. "She's too pink," he says. "And nobody has that much hair."

"You'd be pink," I tell him. "Bollock-naked on a horse."

"The horse is shite too," Frank says, and there he does have a point. It's drawn around the balcony on rails, and it's not bad enough that it glides, but it totters, too, as it corners. The last chimes die away and we watch Godiva wobble back inside for another hour.

Peeping Tom, Lisa is saying, was the only one of the townsfolk who spied on Godiva. "And he was blinded for his trouble."

"Blinded by who?" one of the old women asks eagerly, and Frank laughs. Lisa looks over at us and glares.

"By her husband, was it?" one of the old blokes chips in hopefully.

"Actually," Lisa says above the laughter, "the legend doesn't tell us. Just that he was struck blind. By God, I suppose."

The old people look a little startled by that, and Lisa says, "Excuse me," and walks over to where we're sitting.

"Just piss off, wouldya?" she says to Frank.

"Ah, we're only having some fun, pet. We were just saying how well you're getting on." He looks at me for support, but she never takes her eyes off him and I keep my mouth shut. The OAPs are watching nervously.

"Here." She digs around in her pocket for a moment and then thrusts her hand out under his nose. She's holding a tenner. "Take it," she says.

"Put it away," Frank says.

The note is new and it quivers a little in the breeze.

"Go on, Dad," she says, more softly, and gently he plucks it from her fingers. He takes it in both hands as if studying it, and only when his eyes drop does she give me a look and I nod to let her know it'll be all right. She walks slowly back to her group and I watch her go. She has her hair tied up, but one loose strand flickers across her neck. The old people are still looking worried, and I feel like calling out to them, "It's all right. It wasn't God. It was shame. Tom was blinded by shame."

Instead, I slap my hands on my thighs and say, "Opening time."

I only moved down here last year to be with Karen after we left college, so I don't have that many what you'd call mates in Coventry. The ones I did have, through work and that — the ones I used to watch football with or talk to about cars or holidays or mortgages — I've lost touch with. It wasn't their fault. I just stopped calling them after a bit.

It's not easy, either, meeting new people on the dole. You can't ask them what they do for a living, for starters. "The only thing worse than being unemployed is being nosy," Frank told me the first time we met. "It's a lonely old business, all right, on the dole — all three million of us." He raised his eyebrows meaningfully. We were stood in the queue to sign on and I kept my mouth shut. Frank was a big bloke. Even balding and beer-bellied he looked hard. We shuffled forward over the rubberized floor toward the plastic window in front. Frank was ahead of me, and when he stepped up to the counter he hunched his shoulders like a kid at school not wanting anyone to see his answers. All we were doing was signing our names, but when it was my turn I covered up same as Frank.

That was the second time I'd signed on. The first time was awful. I got home and felt exhausted. It was like a day's work — catching the bus, queuing up, signing my name. I lay down on the couch with the TV on and curled myself into a ball. That was about a fortnight after Karen left.

I didn't remember Frank when he introduced himself, but he said he was Lisa's father. Lisa Chambers. We'd met at a parents' evening.

"Oh, Mr. Chambers," I said, but he stuck out his hand and said, "Frank."

"Chris," I said.

Lisa was a student of mine in the fifth-form biology class I taught last year. I took over as a supply teacher the Christmas before their exams and found they'd covered most of the syllabus apart from sex education. Their previous teacher had got pregnant and couldn't bear to teach them in her condition. "You know how their dirty little minds work," she'd said.

Frank took me down the pub with him and then had me home for dinner. We sat in his kitchen over a cup of tea waiting for Lisa to come home from her summer job at five-thirty. It felt like I hadn't talked to anyone for weeks. We started with football, but by the time we were done I'd told him so much I was embarrassed. I hadn't really talked to anyone about Karen until then. Most of our friends had been mutual and I'd been too ashamed to call them somehow. We'd been seeing each other for two years before she got the research assistantship at Warwick University. Last spring she was offered a Ph.D. place. Now she's sleeping with the head of her lab.

Frank made it easier by telling me stuff too. He said he hadn't worked for nearly two years, since Ford bought Jaguar and rationalized the plant.

"'Rationalized,'" Frank said. "Like it made fuck-all sense to me."

Frank had this whole philosophy of unemployment worked out. How to handle it. Keeping your chin up was his big tip. "Look, there are no jobs round here. You've just got to accept it. All you can do is try and stay busy, make yourself useful, feel like you're worth something." He cooked for Lisa every evening. She was back by then, and she rolled her eyes when she heard that, mimed two fingers down her throat, but Frank kept on. He did the shopping, he said, and the ironing, and pushed the hoover round the house every morning without fail.

"My job now," he said, "is being the best father I can be."

"I hope it's not just a job!" Lisa broke in.

"More like hard bleeding labour," Frank said, and he gave her arm a squeeze.

Since he'd not had one — or even a sniff of one — everything had become a job for Frank. Looking for work was a job, "just not one I'm much good at." Being a good father was a job. Being a good mate. Keeping his chin up was a full-time job.

"Thanks," I told him at the door when I left that night, and he said, "For what? Listen. We have to stick together." He meant the unemployed.

"No, really," I said.

"Here," Frank said. "Let me tell you. You were one of the few who ever encouraged Lisa at that school. Made her want to stay on and try for college."

I tried to tell him it was my job, after all, but he went on.

"She's going to be better than her old man. Don't get me wrong. I'm not one of those fellas who says, 'Why should my kids have more than me?' God knows I want her to have more than this."

Lisa had come up behind him to see me off, and I could see her shifting her weight from foot to foot, embarrassed. I nodded to show I was listening. Frank must have sensed her, though — that or the draught through the open door. "Well, anyway," he said, "she always used to tell me how biology was her favourite subject." That made me feel absurdly happy for a moment, but Lisa just blushed.

The pub is a pit — torn seats, yellowing wallpaper, bulges of damp in the ceiling plaster — but it's empty at lunchtimes and it's got a dartboard. Frank doesn't like crowds, and darts are better than bar billiards because you can play for free. Frank taught me that.

At the bar he pulls out Lisa's tenner, folds it lengthwise, making a sharp crease with his nail, and asks me what I'm having. After a second I say, "Bitter shandy."

"Bugger that," he says. "Two pints of bitter," he tells the girl, and we wait in silence, watching the glasses fill. When she puts them back on the bar, I try to slip her my half, but Frank says, "Gerraway! I'm getting these in."

The barmaid looks at us blankly. "Fine," I say, and then, "Ta," and finally, "Cheers."

We've been coming here right through the summer, every couple of weeks after signing on, and this is the first time either of us has bought the other a drink. I take a sip while Frank pays. I should be buying him one. I got a job offer last week, but I still haven't told Frank and now's not the time. The man's buying me a drink. Besides, it's up north and I don't know if I'll take it yet.

"She made that up," he says now, when we've sat down and he's had a good drink. "Lisa did. About God and that."

"Really?"

"Bastard."

"She thinks on her feet, Frank. She's good at her job." I try to sound bored. Frank doesn't know about Lisa and me.

"She's asking for trouble. That thing about the poll tax is something she just threw in there. She says she has to do something to make it interesting. Says it's boring otherwise. Next thing you know she'll be telling the wrinklies Peeping Tom was getting his leg over."

I take a sip of beer and watch Frank over the rim of my glass as he raises his own. Frank needs a pint after signing on to give himself something to look forward to. He closes his eyes to drink.

Wrinklies is what Frank calls Lisa's OAPs. She says that's rich coming from him. "Don't go lumping your dad with them," he tells her. "I've taken early retirement, see. Early." Frank is forty-six. Lisa told me once that he'll never work again, and for a moment I thought she said he'd never walk again.

When Frank finishes his beer I say, "My shout," and grab the empties quick as I can. We can't afford a tip so we take our glasses up when we're done. Frank taught me that, too. He follows me over to the bar, but I don't give him a chance to pay. Then when the barmaid gives me my change, he says to her, "An' a couple of whiskies, luv."

"That tenner's burned a hole in your pocket," I tell him, and he throws the whisky down without even bothering to take it back to the table. It makes me wince, but he just sighs contentedly.

"Cheers, big ears," he says.

We play darts for a bit, but neither of us can hit a double to save our lives.

"You know what you need," Frank says when he finally gets out. "You need glasses, pal." This is an old one. He's been after me forever to get an eye test. They're free for the unemployed.

"My eyes are fine."

"Next game on it," he says, on his way to the bar for another couple of pints and two more doubles.

"You're on," I say, taking up the darts, but Frank beats me hollow. I've not had more than a pint at a time for weeks, and the whisky's ruining my game.

A couple of Frank's mates, Tony and Don, come in as Frank is finishing me off. "Good arrows," Don calls. Tony has a tightly rolled-up newspaper under his arm, which he waves in our direction. They get their pints and pull up chairs. Don asks, "What's the crack, lads?"

Frank's mates are about the same age as him, and the first time Frank brought me down here they didn't like the look of me. I was young. I had a degree. What the fuck was I doing there? It was as if they didn't expect to see me again, and they hardly bothered to say a word in my direction. They've warmed to me over the weeks, though, especially since they found out I was Lisa's teacher.

"Did you ever teach that Debbie Jackson?" Don wanted to know, and I said yes. Debbie had been in Lisa's class but dropped out for a career as a topless model for the *Sun*. The idea that I'd taught sex education to a page-three girl entertained Frank's friends no end.

Tony's got a big grin on his chops today as he unrolls his newspaper and says, "Got a nice picture of your girlfriend in here, professor." He likes to let on that Debbie had a crush on me. ("Stands to reason. You being an authority figure, teaching her the ways of the world and all that.") He smoothes the paper down and we all lean forward to have a look.

The page won't lie flat, but Debbie is clearly recognizable. She's posed, topless, perched on the front of an ice cream van. She's laughing, wearing bikini bottoms, her head thrown back, about to take a big lick of an ice cream she holds in her hand. Don reads us the caption: "De-lovely Debbie Jackson's ambition is to be a journalist. Here she is getting her first big scoop."

Debbie is all tits and hips, Lisa slim and a little flat-chested.

"Why do they always have to pretend that those girls want another job?" Frank says. "It's like when they ask the beauty queens what they want to be. She's got a job. She's a model. What's she want to be a journalist for?"

Debbie's become a bit of a celebrity in recent weeks. The city holds a Lady Godiva parade every year and the lord mayor usually chooses some local beauty to ride through town in a body stocking. This year, though, a Labour councillor's put her own name forward for the job, because she thinks she can use the ride to protest the poll tax. The *Sun* picked up the story as an example of loony left politics and suggested that Debbie, as a local girl, would be the better choice. Beside the article they printed pictures of

Debbie ("local lovely") and the councillor ("stick to politics").

"Your Lisa should have a go," Tony tells Frank now. He gives Don and me a broad wink. "She's a little cracker."

"What's that supposed to mean?" Frank says. I feel myself tense. Tony stares at his newspaper. "What's that supposed to *mean*?" Frank leans into the table and it rocks. Tony's pint slops a little, and he puts his hand around the glass. "I would die of shame," Frank says, "if that was my daughter riding around starkers. I hope I've brought her up better than that." He looks over at me and tells me to sup up so we can get to the optician's. He raises his glass — it must be two thirds full — and drinks off the rest of his pint. His Adam's apple throbs in his neck, and a little beer runs down his cheeks.

I look at the half pint sitting in front of me and feel sick at the thought of drinking it, but make myself anyway. Wasting it would make Frank wonder what was wrong with me. Don gives us a mock salute as we leave. "See you in a fortnight," he says, meaning the next time we sign on. "Same bat-time, same bat-bar."

Tony looks up, briefly, and goes back to studying his newspaper.

I was all right sitting down, but when we come up the steps I reel a little from the booze, and Frank has to take my arm for a moment. It occurs to me that I won't be able to tell him about the job now, and I lean on him in relief. I wouldn't be able to make a decision about it in this state and I don't trust myself to say it right. I'd start on about the job, but I'd end up telling him about Lisa and me.

Instead, I say I'm busting for a piss, and he stands guard while I go behind a skip.

I often wonder what made Frank pick me. Of course, we've got more in common than Lisa or just being unemployed. We're both big footy fans, and I go round there most Sunday afternoons to watch the game. When Frank talks about his old job he never says he was "sacked" or "fired" or "laid off." He says he was "given his marching orders" or he "took an early bath" — like a footballer who's got sent off. When I talk about Karen, I say she "kicked me into touch."

What we really have in common is that Frank's been sacked and I've been dumped. In the beginning I thought Frank's philosophy — keep busy, believe in yourself — would help me get over Karen.

I haven't talked to her for two months. She's still with him, her boss. He must be twenty years older than her. I suppose I've been hanging around all summer waiting to see what'll happen there. "You'll get over her," Frank tells me from time to time, but some nights, when I can't sleep, I walk out to the university and look up at her window. I wrote and asked her to explain it to me once and she just said she hoped we could be friends. I don't believe in that, though. I don't think it's possible — staying friends after you've been lovers. It's just one of those modern myths.

I suppose Frank's lonely himself — his wife died five

years ago. But he likes to see himself as a thinker. "Boredom," he says, "is our black hole. The centre of the unemployed universe. It'll suck you up if you're not watching." He's started to go down the library and the museum, but he doesn't like to go alone, and he doesn't know anyone else who'll go with him.

Lisa says her father's just a snob. "He likes to hang out with a better class of unemployed people." Meaning me.

The optician's is behind the cathedral, and as we're walking between the new cathedral that they built in the fifties and the ruins of the old one bombed in the war, we see Lisa again with another party. Frank waves but she ignores him, and he makes us follow her inside and lurk on the fringe of the group. She smiles at me a couple of times, but when she sees her father looking she scowls. The walk has cleared my head some, but dealing with Lisa and Frank is too much and I take a seat in a pew. The cathedral is cool, almost cold, after the sunlight outside.

Lisa is telling the OAPs about the tapestry of Christ — the world's largest tapestry — which covers one entire wall of the cathedral. It shows Christ seated, but from straight on the chair is hidden by his robes and the perspective is lost. It looks as though Christ is standing, as though his body is a long oval. Frank says he looks pregnant, but to me, when I can get my focus, it looks like Christ has a thorax and an abdomen. He looks like a great, stinging insect. That's the biology teacher in me.

Lisa points out details. Her suit jacket rides up as she raises her hand, and I catch a glimpse of white blouse at her waist. The tapestry was woven in France, where it took two hundred women over a million hours to complete.

"Waste of effing time," Frank whispers.

Suddenly I think I'm going to throw up, right here in the cathedral. I have to put my head between my knees to steady myself.

Lisa begins to lead her group back outside, and Frank helps me up. At the door she stops and slips some coins into the donations box. Most of the tour party does the same, but Frank and I walk past quickly. Lisa gets a special allowance for this from the tourist board. It's by arrangement with the cathedral, a way of raising some revenue for the upkeep of the place.

"Fucking sheep," Frank says as we walk away. He hates the OAPs because they're allowed to do nothing.

The first time Lisa came by my flat was about two months ago. It was a Monday, her day off, she said, and she was out cycling. I told her I could see that. She was flushed and wearing cycling shorts and a tight white T-shirt. She asked if she could have a glass of water and I helped her pull her bike inside and she followed me upstairs.

"Don't look at the mess," I said, hurrying ahead of her to push my job applications into a neat pile and cover them with the phone book. I wasn't sure whether I was worried about what Lisa might think if she saw them or what she might tell Frank.

I offered her a seat, but she preferred to bend over and study my bookshelves.

"You have a great collection," she said.

"I've not got much to do with myself but read," I called back from the kitchen. "You're welcome to borrow any of them."

"I'd like that."

When I came back she pretended not to be looking at the photograph of Karen on one of the shelves and I pretended not to have caught her. I passed her her glass. My fingers were wet with condensation and I dried them on my jeans.

The receptionist at the optician's is on the phone when we arrive. She is perched behind her desk, twirling a pen in her long fingers. We loiter under the bright fluorescent lights and I try on a few frames and pull faces at Frank. I'm trying to distract him. The girl is clearly making a personal call, and I can see Frank getting tense. It's not that we don't have the time, of course, but Frank hates to see a job done badly. "There's no reason," he hisses. "Not with so many people in need of work."

Eventually she looks up, covers the mouthpiece, and asks brightly if she can help us. Frank tells her I'd like an eye test.

"They're free if you're unemployed, right?" I ask, and Frank looks daggers at me.

"Uh-huh," the girl says and tells us to take a seat. The optician is with someone. She goes back to her conversation. Frank flips through the pile of magazines on the table — back issues of *The Optician* — and finally sits back, crosses his arms, and glares at the girl.

I nudge him and whisper, "Doctor, recently I keep imagining every woman I see naked. On a horse." It's a stupid thing to say and makes me think that I'm really drunk, but Frank just grunts. The receptionist looks over at our whispering, but he stares her down.

Frank hasn't looked for work in a newspaper or at the job centre for six months. In one week, he's told me, he went to twelve interviews and didn't get a single offer, and he doesn't believe in job creation anymore. "There are no new ones round here," he says, "just fewer and fewer of the old ones." What he does now is to watch other people at work in shops or restaurants, wherever he goes, and decide if he could do their job better than them. He lives for bad service — especially if he thinks someone is treating him badly because he's unemployed. Quick as a flash he'll write off a letter of complaint, and always at the end, often in a P.S., he'll offer his own services. He thinks if he makes the complaint vicious enough, they'll sack someone and consider him for a job. I find myself defending people just to stop him sending a letter that'll do him no good and only land someone else in hot water.

The receptionist, having finally finished her call, says the optician will see me now and gestures toward a staircase behind her. Frank makes a big song and dance and insists on coming with me, and she smiles blandly and says, "If you like."

"That was nice of her," I say as we go up. "Wasn't it?"

"The universe," Frank whispers back darkly, "is finite and shrinking, buddy boy. There's no one creating nothing, just remember that."

Lisa told me that she loved me last week, and then she asked me if I loved her. I said she was a lovely girl.

"You're still in love with her," she said.

"Debbie?" I said, but she was serious.

"Karen!"

"No."

She looked me in the eye, saw I was telling the truth, and it seemed to satisfy her. I was disappointed. This isn't the nitrogen cycle, I wanted to tell her. It's not photosynthesis. You don't have to take my word for it.

She likes to come to me in the morning of her day off, before I get up, and crawl in beside me. After we make love, she sleeps. Her lie-in, she calls it, and after an hour I slip out and bring her a cup of tea.

I'm twenty-four and she's seventeen. I think Lisa sees our lovemaking as a way of growing up, although I know I'm not her first. She's conscious, too, that somehow her having a job and my being unemployed has closed the gap. Besides, she likes the sneaking around. We hardly ever talk about her father. The subject makes me uncomfortable. "Bor-ring," she says. But Frank's only boring when we talk about him. When we don't, when he's this shared unspoken thing, she likes it. It's romantic. She thinks the secrecy brings us together.

"Maybe he already knows," Lisa said once, and then, when she saw the look on my face, "Just teasing."

A little later, she asked, "You could get a job, right?"

"Lisa," I said. "I'm a teacher. It's the summer holidays."

"But next year?"

"Next year? Yeah, probably."

"Thought so," she said, and there was a glint of triumph in her voice.

Sometimes Lisa makes me wonder why I ever thought she was such a promising student. I can't tell her, but I wish she could just see that I sleep with her every Monday for something to do.

The optician parks Frank on a stool at the back and points me toward the chair in the centre of the room. I'm still feeling the effects of the beer and whisky, and when he asks me to read the letters on the screen I'm not sure if my eyes are that bad or if it's the booze. Next he switches the overhead light off and makes me look at a lighted board of letters and symbols while he slips the heavy lens support over my head. In the darkness, perched on the chair with the odd weight on my head, I'm beginning to feel the room spin.

It's quiet in the office, just the optician's voice asking me, "Better, worse, or the same?" as he clips lenses into place, and the sound of Frank's breathing. A couple of times I can't say if my vision is better, worse, or the same and I make up an answer. My mouth tastes foul.

This must have been what it was like for the peasants waiting for Godiva to ride by, I think. Sitting in the dark, refusing to look out and shame her. Just listening to the horse. Then I think, maybe she wasn't all that pretty after all. Maybe that part's the legend. Perhaps Tom looked out and was blinded by her plainness.

Frank farts somewhere behind me — it's soft and so prolonged that he must be faking it somehow — but after a moment I can't help myself. I laugh so hard I lose my balance and have to put out a hand to grab the optician.

"Don't waste my time," he hisses out of the darkness. He puts his face close to mine and says, "Some of us have work to do." I steady myself and sit still. I used to teach the eye.

The optician clicks another lens into place — the sound is dry and precise — and the tiny letters jump into a focus that seems almost supernatural. "Better, worse, the same?" he says, and I tell him, "Much better." I hear him make a final scratch with his pen and he flicks the lights back on.

Gleaming in his white coat, he tells me I'm short-sighted and need glasses. He asks me what I do, and after a moment's hesitation I tell him I'm a teacher. He looks hard at me and says, "Right."

He tells me that I qualify for a discount of twenty pounds on the lenses and that I can choose frames from the selection downstairs. His voice is flat, and when he's finished he turns his back on us as if we'd never been there.

Frank and I go look at frames. He's embarrassed that this free trip is going to cost me money, but I'm still smarting from the optician's voice and also somehow elated by the memory of my improved eyesight. I try on a few pairs, but the national health ones make me look like one of my students and I find myself picking the more expensive frames. I look like someone else with each pair I try, and eventually I find one I like. I stare at myself and think, That's how I want to look. It's an odd moment of recognition. I wear the frames over to the girl at her desk and she smiles and says, "They suit you."

She pulls out a calculator and pecks away at it with her bright nails until she works out that the lenses and the frames together will cost me just under ninety quid.

"What about the discount?" Frank wants to know, but she tells me that she was including the discount. "Bugger that," he says. But the girl looks at me expectantly, and I say, "Fine."

Frank starts to say something, but then turns and walks away to look at sunglasses. The girl gives me a business card and says that the specs will be ready tomorrow after lunch.

Frank is wearing a pair of dark glasses with the price tag dangling over his nose when I go over to him. He's bent down, peering at himself in one of the little mirrors. When I appear behind him, he waggles his eyebrows at me in the mirror. It looks comic, his bushy eyebrows above the glasses. I say, "Let's go," and he takes the glasses off and blinks hard in the sunlight.

"You don't have to pick them up if you don't want," Frank says out in the street, but the idea of leaving the glasses there seems somehow shocking to me. Now that I know what I'm missing, it would be impossible.

"It's fine," I tell him.

"No, really. He's a wanker, that optician. Just don't go back. All right?"

"Forget it."

I ask him if he wants to play some table tennis. Frank is a demon at table tennis, beating me consistently with undiminished delight, but he just shakes his head. "How 'bout going down the museum?" In the end, he suggests going back to the cathedral and climbing the old spire, the only bit of it left standing after the war.

"It's a beautiful day," he says. "The view'll be something else."

Our UB40s get us in free and I follow Frank up the twisty staircase, peering at the graffiti along the way. The narrow windows in the walls let in enough light for me to make out hearts and arrows and penises and balls. I'm relieved we didn't run into Lisa again outside the cathedral. Her tour circles every forty minutes or so.

Frank counts the stairs softly in time with his breathing. "Two hundred and eight," he says at the top, and we step out onto the balcony. The spire extends another twenty feet above us, but this is as high as we can go. We walk around slowly, and it's so clear we can see for miles. The breeze is stronger up here, and looking into it makes me blink. Frank points out his house, and the floodlights at Highfield Road where the City play, and the pub and the job centre and the road that leads out of town to the old plant. He points and I squint and say, "Oh yeah."

Now that I'm sobering up, I think I should have told Frank when I was drunk. Told him about this new job. Teaching in Manchester. Starting in a couple of weeks.

Not that the details matter. Not that he needs me to tell him now. My mind is made up. I stare out at the view.

"The world is your lobster," I say — an old Monty Python line — but Frank only looks puzzled.

I lean over one side and look down at the pitted head of a gargoyle. The university should be out there somewhere, but I can't make it out. Below and to my right the crosses in a cemetery look like a box of matches someone has dropped.

I feel like I should be trying to memorize the view.

The last time I walked out past Karen's I stepped quietly over the gravel of the car park below her window, placing my feet carefully and gradually letting my weight settle on them. I had begun a letter to her, something to say I thought we could be friends now if she wanted, but I'd never posted it. It wasn't that love for Lisa replaced my love for Karen. It was the fact that I didn't love Lisa and slept with her anyway that changed everything.

On an impulse I threw a stone up against Karen's window and immediately stepped back into the shadows, my heart pounding, staring up at the drawn curtains. But no one came. I hoped they were in there, still, listening, their ears ringing from the snap of the stone on the glass, afraid to look out. But there was as much chance that the room was empty and that they were at his house.

Frank's looking over another side down into the walls of the cathedral itself, and I go over and stand with him. It's just after five and offices are emptying. There are figures in suits walking home through the ruins, and in the late afternoon sun they throw elongated shadows and move across the ground in complicated antlike patterns.

A tour party moves among the workers, but I can't tell if it's Lisa's. All the guides wear the same outfits. We watch as the group is shepherded from the cross of charred beams salvaged from the bombing to the site of the old altar.

"You have to imagine a wooden roof," Frank says in a falsetto, and I realize he is reciting Lisa's script. "The cathedral didn't take a direct hit, but when the buildings on either side were bombed, the heat was enough to cause the timbers to start to smoke and burst into flames. They collapsed into the cathedral and the fire melted the leaded windows, destroying all but a few panes of the beautiful stained glass." In his normal voice he says, "You'll be moving on, then?"

I nod.

"Have you told Lisa?"

Oddly, I'm not surprised. But I can't think of anything to say. All I can think is how unsurprised I am.

"Just going to leave her?" he says. "Without a word of goodbye. What a fucking disgrace." When I don't look up, he says, "Not good enough for you, was she?"

I almost reply to that, but something in his breathing makes me stop and listen. It's short and ragged. I think, *he's crying*. But nothing in the world would make me look. This goes on for a couple of minutes. I watch the tour party straggle back and forth and finally stop beneath the spire.

"Too bleeding old," Frank says at last. "They won't climb it."

We see their faces turn up toward us, and Frank waves. He waves like a kid, shaking his forearm back and forth. The sleeve of his nylon anorak makes a sound like panting.

"Come on," he says, and I join him, feeling foolish until those below begin to wave back. If I had my new glasses I think I'd be able to make out their faces, although the thought of leaning over the edge with ninety pounds' worth of glasses hooked over my ears gives me a moment of vertigo.

The old folks are getting tired of waving, and a few of their arms are falling. The guide is holding a hand up to shield her eyes, trying to make out against the sky who's up here.

"Come 'ere," Frank says, and he takes my arm roughly and pulls me back against the spire. He leans his back and head against the cool, rough stone for a moment and then thrusts himself to the edge and spits.

We stay up there until it begins to get dark. It's the end of August and the nights are already beginning to draw in. I watch streetlights come on below us, pink at first and then amber as they warm up. Finally we hear someone shout up from below that they're closing the spire. In the dark on the way down, Frank leads and I put my hand on his shoulder.

BUOYANCY

THEY USED TO SHOW me a large earthenware jar in one corner of the garden and tell me that was where my great-uncle drowned himself. Like a child I believed them. The jar was certainly large enough for me to drown in. I could have crouched down inside it and been perfectly hidden. But a grown man would have had to be a contortionist to fit himself inside.

I can't remember who told me the story first, but soon the whole family — all the uncles and aunts — knew I lived in fear of that jar. My cousins used to taunt me with it. Ah Wei, in particular, loved to sweep me up in his arms and dangle me, struggling and screaming, over the mouth of the jar, until I kicked so hard my sandals fell off into the darkness and my bare heels scuffed the neck.

Of course, I believed the jar was haunted. I imagined rows of teeth just inside the rim. How else to explain that nothing dropped into the jar ever made a sound of hitting bottom? How else to explain, once the rainy season started, that nothing floated in it, not even leaves? It was the resting place of Great-Uncle's ghost. Sometimes I thought the jar was bottomless, just a deep hole straight down to Great-Uncle's grave. At other times I'd think of him squeezed and folded up inside, with his teeth pressed against his knees, coiled up, ready to spring out.

The rainy season went on for weeks. Every evening at dusk the rain would begin to fall, and every morning the jar would be a little fuller. After about two weeks, you could see the shiny black surface of the water deep inside the jar. After about a month, it was high enough to reflect my terror-stricken face.

I began to imagine Great-Uncle swimming more and more agitatedly below the surface. He would be picking up speed, twisting and turning. His skin would be milky white, but his hair would be slicked back with Bryl Creem like all the men in the family. And he'd feel his way with polyps for fingers, like the horns of a snail.

I began to live in dread of the night the rains would finally fill the jar and set him free. He'd come slithering over the lip and thrash around angrily in the sodden grass.

But after more than two months of rains the jar still wasn't full. Water, I suppose, evaporated so quickly from that wide neck. The rains finished for a year, and when they came around again I no longer believed in Great-Uncle's ghost.

Grandfather had brought Great-Uncle over to Malaya from China to help in the family business. There was a gap of almost two decades between them; grandfather's eldest sons were not much younger than Great-Uncle.

It might have been that the sons resented this new uncle. That's one version. But most people say Great-Uncle just didn't know how to do business. Customers certainly liked him, but instead of selling them anything he took to offering them tea and brandy. Afternoons of drinking became evenings of gambling, and Great-Uncle, perhaps because he was host, invariably lost. He was still only in his early twenties, and most of Grandfather's customers were much older than him, so he felt that it was an honor for them to drink with him and take his money at all.

"Not that it was *his* money," as First Aunty says.

Grandfather soon sent him packing to a tin mine we owned out in the country. There was nothing for Great-Uncle to do, but there was no one with enough money to gamble with him, so Grandfather was satisfied. Grandfather even gave him a brand-new bicycle, which eased his own conscience and made Great-Uncle feel he was being promoted.

He would cycle home every Saturday night to eat with the family, and every Sunday morning he would line the young uncles and aunties up to take turns on his handlebars as he careened across the compound. Grandfather would come out and sit on the porch swing to read his newspaper and never once flinch, no matter how close the bicycle came. When he finished he would hand the paper to Great-Uncle and it would be time to leave.

Back at the mine, the old foreman, Hang, viewed

Great-Uncle with distrust. It was never clear whether he thought Great-Uncle was there to spy on him or he was there to spy on Great-Uncle. But Hang attached himself to his new manager tenaciously. He dedicated himself to keeping Great-Uncle away from the miners and the mine machinery, even the ore. Great-Uncle took to riding laps around the mine on his bicycle just to get away from Hang and then cycling off down jungle tracks to explore the surrounding country.

That was how he found the old mining pool. He'd started riding down a little dirt track and heard shouts and laughter ahead. He stood up on the pedals to see and then rode harder until he shot out onto the banks of a huge pool. It was cool in those waters, and boys and workers came out from the mines and villages nearby to swim. Great-Uncle had never seen anyone swimming before. He slammed on his brakes. Obviously he couldn't swim — no one in the family could — but he sat and watched for hours, staring at the patterns made by swimmers on the water, and gradually, after many days, he learned how by watching. Finally one afternoon he undressed, walked into the water, and began to swim. Every day he went back.

Grandfather got to hear of it — he had his sources — but he did nothing. Swimming was a pointless pastime as far as he was concerned, but at least Great-Uncle was fearless in it. The pool was only a few hundred yards wide and there were no currents, but Great-Uncle was the only one who would swim across. It wasn't the distance so much as the depth that frightened others off.

The old mine had been an open-cast pit and nearly three hundred men had worked on its sides. People who'd seen it at the time used to say that you could stand at the top and men at the bottom looked like ants. The pit had been abandoned when it became too expensive to pump out the water. It was said the water wasn't just deep enough to drown you, it was deep enough to swallow you up. Your body might never be found. It might never stop sinking.

Then one day Great-Uncle borrowed a pair of welder's goggles from the factory. He took them with him into the water, slipped them over his head, and dived beneath the surface. When he opened his eyes, the tiny pocket of air trapped in the goggles allowed him to focus. He was the first swimmer in that pool and perhaps the first in that whole country to be able to see clearly underwater.

For the other swimmers he lent the goggles to, it was interesting but not incredible. After all, what was there to see? There were no fish in the pond, and the bottom was black with mud. But to Great-Uncle it was fascinating. When Grandfather found the goggles and snatched them back, Great-Uncle got some glass and cut up an old inner tube and made himself another pair. He would sit in the shallows staring at the swimmers for hours. He lay on his back with his hands thrust deep into the mud, looking up at them flying overhead, until he lost his grip in the ooze and floated to the surface. To the children, he said it was like standing on your head, seeing the world upside-down. First Aunty remembers them all trying it, waiting in line for a ride on the handlebars one Sunday morning, six children catching a glimpse of their uncle cycling by upside-down before they rolled over into the dust of the compound.

He began to swim out farther, into the centre of the pool. He spent whole days lying facedown on the water over the deepest part of the old pit. There was nothing to see, people would tell him, only darkness. It was true, but for the first time he was seeing the darkness clearly and not as a blur. He almost felt he could see the particles of darkness, the little motes of blackness.

He took to lying in the centre of the pool well into the night. He would float facedown for a minute and then roll over onto his back and rest, catching his breath, staring up at the night sky. Then he would roll back under again. His body went numb in the cold water. His vision was partly blocked by the goggles, and his ears were filled only with the sound of his own breathing. There were times when he didn't know which way he was facing, whether he was breathing or holding his breath.

No one knew what he was thinking about for so many hours in the water. At the house, Grandfather forbade any talk on the subject. But the young uncles and aunts whispered among themselves. Third Uncle says he thought Great-Uncle had a plan, that he knew there was still tin in the mine and was thinking of some way of mining it underwater. He was just thinking of a way to earn his fortune and make the family proud of him. But First Aunty says Great-Uncle always gave Third Uncle the longest bicycle rides of anyone.

For whatever reason, Great-Uncle was becoming obsessed with reaching the bottom.

He began a series of experiments. He started by waterproofing a torch, sealing it in a bottle, and lowering it into the darkness. He could see the lamp descending, but it showed him nothing but more blackness, a clearer darkness. He lost torch after torch as they vanished from sight. He learned to dive on the surface, folding his body and raising his legs until he dropped down with the falling lights, but still they vanished without any sign of the bottom.

He practised until he could fall far into the water, but it was never far enough. He built a small raft and piled it with stones. Large ones he would hug to his chest, letting himself be pulled down, only releasing them when his lungs were bursting. Small ones he loaded into sacks, plunging after them. Each time he felt his breath leaving him, he stretched out a hand in the darkness. But his numb fingers never touched the bottom.

Once he tried to make a buoy to anchor the raft. He tethered an empty oil drum to it with a rock for ballast, but he misjudged the weight. The drum sank out of sight, almost dragging the raft with it, and a moment later a great rush of bubbles engulfed him. When he hauled the drum back to the surface it was crushed in two.

All he could think of was a creature, some malevolent water spirit large enough to crush oil drums in its teeth, lying curled at the bottom of the pond.

It was a frightening discovery, but it didn't frighten

Great-Uncle. It angered him. It maddened him. The existence of such a creature meant that the pond was not truly his.

He bought great lengths of cord and began fashioning huge nets. The work was long, but by calculating the size of an animal with jaws wide enough to seize an oil drum, he knew he could leave the holes in the net large. He sat in the shallows each day tying his net together and each night lay out over the depths, staring into the darkness. Every time in whatever part of the pool he sent down an oil drum, he pulled it up crushed.

It took hours to lower the net into the water. The weight of the cord and the stones needed to sink it almost swamped his raft. He lay his net in a tight circle in the deepest part of the pond and began sending down oil drums. When the first air bubbles began boiling to the surface, he went over the side with a huge slab of rock clutched to his chest.

The darkness was alight. Here and there along the net he'd tied torch bottles, and as he plummeted with his huge stone, it was like falling into the stars. The darkness had never been clearer, the blackness never sharper. He plunged for what seemed like hours, marveling at his lung capacity. He never saw the creature, but he began to see his oil drums sinking ahead of him. Then he knew he'd held on too long. He was too deep. He let go of his stone to rise but he was disoriented. The surface looked as distant as the bottom. He didn't know which way to turn. He felt himself falling and tried to turn back but it was too late. He fell faster and faster until at last the bottom came into sight. There it was in the distance. He came closer, accelerating through the darkness, until it stretched away all around him. And he crashed against it.

He found himself on the surface, looking up at the stars. He lay there for hours, concentrating on staying afloat, staring into the night sky until it began to flow over his head and the light of dawn washed over him. That's how the first swimmers found him. He had suffered an embolism, the English doctors told him later. One of his lungs had ruptured. He had surfaced too fast, and the reduced pressure had caused the air in his right lung to expand until it burst. It felt like his chest was smashed. But he'd found the monster he'd been looking for below. The pressure that had crushed his oil drums.

He never swam again. Grandfather was convinced he was mad. The uncles and aunties all remember Grandfather coming home from the hospital and telling them Great-Uncle was sick. A brain rupture, he said, and none of them dared to ask what he meant. When Great-Uncle came out of the hospital the children all demanded that he come home and live with them. Grandfather acquiesced, but Great-Uncle was a disappointment. He was still sick and his playfulness was gone. In the end, when the children had lost interest in him and Grandfather had tried everything, including sorcery, to restore him, the family wrote from China to suggest that Great-Uncle return there. A wife had been found.

None of the uncles or aunties can even remember her name, but it seems she was the widow of a herbalist in a village near our family home in China. She had learned her husband's trade and wanted to continue it now that he was dead, but she needed a man to conduct business for her with other men. She knew Great-Uncle had been ill, but this was no bar to her. She promised the family she would restore him and a bargain was struck.

So Great-Uncle was set up in business again and for a while all was well. He put on flesh and his body healed, although any exercise was still hard. If he had been mad, he recovered his wits too. He was a good advertisement for his wife's remedies and for a time business boomed.

His returning health, however, did not make Great-Uncle any better a businessman. He had too many friends among his customers and began another round of tea and brandy evenings, with a little mahjong thrown in for good measure. And he still lost.

It was an expensive habit, this gambling, his wife found. In vain she sought a cure. She mixed herbs in his dishes to bring him luck. She mixed herbs to make him vomit whenever he drank alcohol. Nothing could purge his losing. In the end, she quietly economized on the more exotic items in her stock — shark's teeth and mother-of-pearl. It didn't take long for the rumours to harm business. Besides, Great-Uncle's bad luck was well known. It was not an auspicious sign.

He did what he could. He curtailed his gambling sessions. His friends were understanding, but they all knew the quality of his brandy had been rapidly declining. They came forward and offered him advice before they left — the name of a man to borrow from. With more money the shelves could be restocked and faith restored.

He did as he was told. The money was spent on

Chinese New Year, a long string of firecrackers hanging down from the roof, a great feast for visitors, and not one, not two, but three troupes of lion-dancers tumbling and charging through the shop. Good fortune and prosperity were demonstrated to all.

The next day he fell ill. It finished business. Many well-wishers came through the shop, but no one bought anything. For a few days people loitered before the store, waiting to see if it would be his wife or he who opened the doors. But by the time he finally felt strong enough to rise, it was too late. Only small boys and a few dogs still hovered outside. They scattered in surprise at the sight of him.

Grandfather arrived the night before the debt came due. He greeted his sister-in-law but never came near his younger brother. He didn't speak to him or touch him, and in the morning he was gone before Great-Uncle awoke. Not a word of the debt had been spoken, but Great-Uncle knew where Grandfather had gone and that he would never return. That was when he sent his wife out marketing — a feast for his brother was what he told her, and she obeyed him.

He spent the next hour carrying water from the village well into his house to fill their water jar. It was a huge jar and held enough water for a whole week. He went slowly because of his health and stopped frequently with the two buckets swaying gently from the yoke across his shoulders. At one time or another, he saw nearly every one of his neighbors and wished them good day.

No one, incidentally, saw him spill a drop. There

were not even any dark patches on the wooden steps of the house. It was hard work for a man who'd been inactive for so long, and he would have been drenched with perspiration.

He placed a chair beside the jar and hung his shirt on it. He took his old pair of goggles down from the shelf and climbed onto the chair. Then he must have lifted himself carefully over the lip and slid in head first. The jar was too narrow for him to turn his shoulders. He would have been able to see nothing but darkness, but he could have felt all around and beneath him the rough walls and floor of the jar closing in on him.

Finally his fingertips would have begun to explore the darkness, feeling it out, finding it exactly as he had always known it would be.

THE SILVER SCREEN

FROM THE END of the Second World War until the outbreak of the insurgency in 1948, the fourteenth Kuala Lumpur branch of the Malayan Communist party held its meetings in the Savoy Cinema on Brickfields Street.

The owner of the cinema, Mr. Ming, had joined the party during the Japanese occupation. In those days, he had cycled to work at his father's rubber plantation on the outskirts of the town. Every morning he would join the line of workers and schoolchildren in front of the Japanese sentry at Pudu jail. They would all dismount at a respectful distance from the sentry, wheel their bicycles to his post, bow, wheel them on, and remount at an equally respectful distance beyond. All this under the eyes of the severed heads lined up along the walls of the jail.

More heads were sure to be added whenever an informer was standing beside the sentry. Informers were distinguished by the brown burlap sacks with ragged eyeholes that they wore over their heads to avoid identification. On mornings when informers were at the guard post, Mr. Ming bowed and then stood for a moment before those eyeholes while they appraised him. He felt his scalp prickle with the stares from the walls of the jail. He used to say he never believed the war was over until he saw a line of heads on the wall, each covered in a sack. 'Someone pulled the sacks off after a day, but then they could have been anyone's heads,' he said. 'And then the British took them down.'

Even before he became a communist, Mr. Ming had little respect for the British. In his eyes, their rapid retreat through Malaya and their ignominious flight from Singapore had tarnished their reputation irreparably. His desire for Malayan independence stemmed as much from a wish for self-rule as from a conviction that the British no longer deserved to govern. 'The Japanese, at least,' he told his friends, 'were famous for their cruelty. All the British are famous for is cricket.'

Everyone on the central committee of the fourteenth branch knew Mr. Ming, but like everyone else, he had a code name. Communist code names in the late forties weren't very imaginative. Mr. Chen, the butcher, was known as the Cockerel. Mr. Ho, the rickshaw driver, was the Foot. Mr. Kuk, the fruit seller, was Shorty. In the Chinese community at that time everyone was a communist or a communist sympathizer, and code names were meant more for notoriety than secrecy. Mr. Ming's code name was the Duke.

This had come about after Ming complained to the artist, Lee, who painted the posters for all his films. He stood outside the cinema one evening watching Lee take down one huge canvas advertising *Westward Ho* and replace it with another for *Stagecoach*. Both starred John

Wayne, but the likenesses of him on the two posters bore no resemblance to each other. They both showed a distinctly Asian man in a Stetson, but that wasn't what Mr. Ming was complaining about.

'Ai-yeu,' he called up as Lee struggled with the huge canvases. 'How are my customers to know that their favourite actor is in both films? You draw a different face each time.' The canvas that Lee was hanging was rolled up like a carpet and stretched across the whole length of the Savoy's façade, nearly twenty feet. He was perched on a long plank running between two rickety bamboo ladders and he was in no mood for an argument. If he shouted he was sure he would fall. As it was, he was convinced that Ming's cries from the street would shake the ladders loose and make the plank jump beneath his feet. He clenched his teeth and finished hanging the poster.

On the ground, Mr. Ming was becoming more and more incensed by this silence, which he took for arrogance. 'Think you're an artist?' he cried. 'Think again! My grandma could paint a better John Wayne.'

When he got down Lee was apologetic. 'Sorry, sorry,' he said. 'I can't help it. I can't paint a face without a model and I can't paint the same face without the same model. John Wayne is sometimes my father, sometimes my uncle, sometimes the boy who brings me my paints.'

This was how Mr. Ming decided that he would be John Wayne. On the pretext of overseeing Lee's work, he became his model. The idea of his own image ten feet high across his cinema was appealing to him. He thought of the great revolutionary paintings of Lenin and Mao and the Man of Steel that he had seen pictures of in communist newspapers.

In time, he found that the affairs of business limited his opportunities for visiting Lee and he had the young artist sit in on meetings of the communist cell to make sketches for his posters. In this way, other members of the party became immortalized. Mr. Chen became the model for Gary Cooper and Humphrey Bogart. Mr. Ho doubled for Charlie Chaplin — a personal favorite. Mr. Kuk, because of his stature, was a natural choice for Audie Murphy, Peter Lorre, and James Cagney. The communists were all secretly interested in the way they were depicted, but of course no one referred openly to the paintings unless to joke, 'I was recognized in the street again last night. A young girl asked me for my autograph! I think she'd make a good Lauren Bacall.' There was an unwritten law that during meetings Lee would be ignored, while the serious business of world communism was conducted. Yet on certain evenings — the night that Lee was sketching his poster of Henry Fonda in *The Grapes of Wrath*, for instance — the communists would argue longer and more passionately, with more sweeping strokes of the hand, their heads held higher and their brows creased deeper.

On the other hand, no one would look up from his food the night that Lee was trying to get a likeness of Sydney Greenstreet. They all held their bowls of rice that much closer to their lips and waved their chopsticks before their faces as they talked.

As for Lee, he paid more attention to his sketches than politics. It wasn't easy capturing the details he needed and he had to work fast. Sometimes he would find that he had concentrated so hard on his work that he had no idea what had been discussed or even who had spoken. These were hardly ideal working conditions, but he felt pleased now when the Duke came out to watch him hang a new poster and stood silently in the street, nodding with satisfaction.

Lee was rarely addressed by the communists except perhaps to be told where to sit, and was never expected to speak himself. The only sounds he was permitted were the quick sighs of his pencil strokes and the occasional scratching of his knife paring a finer point. Some evenings he didn't even wait until the end of the discussion. If he had enough sketches for his poster he would collect up his pencils and paper and, bowing quickly to the others, leave to catch the last reel of that night's feature. The Savoy was an open-air cinema — four high walls with no roof and a huge canvas screen stretched out against the night sky — and Lee loved to imagine that what he was seeing was the lives of the gods. It was his habit, as he watched, to leave the sketchbook open on his lap and by the end of the evening he would have covered the page unconsciously with half-formed figures.

He had his own heroes, of course, just like the communists, and for himself he reserved the role of Johnny Weissmuller, holding up a small shaving mirror to sketch himself as Tarzan, Lord of the Jungle.

In 1948, when Chin Peng, the chairman of the Malayan politburo, authorized the first attacks on British plantation owners, the fourteenth branch of the Kuala Lumpur

Communist party went into the jungle along with five thousand other communist fighters. Many, like Chin Peng himself, had fought alongside the British against the Japanese occupying forces three years earlier. Chin Peng, indeed, had been flown to London to march past King George in the victory parade. Mr. Kuk and Mr. Chen had both served with distinction in the war and Mr. Ho had for a time been a prisoner of the Japanese, but it was Mr. Ming who took the lead in their platoon. The others accepted this in part because Ming had always been the most prosperous among them but also because they based themselves in the jungle near the plantation owned by Ming's father. 'Our first Liberated Area,' he called it in his opening address to the platoon. The workers from the plantation could be relied upon to turn a blind eye to their movements and also to supply food and medicines as the campaign wore on.

For many months the Duke, Mr. Cooper, Mr. Chaplin, Mr. Murphy, and about twenty young men from the Brickfields area waged a successful campaign against the British and American plantations surrounding the small Ming estate. The Silver Screen Brigade, as they dubbed themselves, was able to harry traffic with impunity and walk at ease into the villages in their immediate area.

Their greatest success in the early days of the Emergency — the authorities were forbidden from referring to it as a war for insurance purposes — was an ambush of a British foot patrol. They picked an isolated bend in a forest path and in the ditch to one side planted sharpened stakes. When the patrol came level with their position they attacked from the other side of the track, driving the British into the ditch. One man was cut down in the first exchange of fire and several more were badly wounded in the ditch. The Duke was all for charging the British, but Mr. Cooper shook his head slightly. The communist practice was to stay hidden in the jungle and avoid major confrontations. The Duke would have argued, but Mr. Cooper slapped him on the back and cried, 'Good shot.' In a moment the whole platoon was applauding. All the British heard was a distant cheering.

The dead man, Lance Corporal Burroughs of the Welsh Guards, better known as 'Boom-boom' Burroughs, the promising British welterweight — so named for the sound he made as he landed his punches on opponents — lay in the track for two hours before his body could be recovered. His death warranted a front-page story in the *Straits Times* and a small black framed box on the sports pages of the *Daily Telegraph*.

Lee, meanwhile, had lost his job as a poster painter. He had arrived by bicycle at the Savoy one evening with his new canvas draped over his shoulder only to find the iron-grille doors padlocked and the foyer dark. He stood in the street for several minutes sniffing the reassuring smell of peanuts and coconut milk from the hawker stall rolled against the back wall. Eventually he slipped around the side of the building and laid his poster gently in the lane. He propped his bicycle against the wall and stood on the saddle to climb over and drop into the shady auditorium. He found the ladders in the usual place under the stairs to Mr. Ming's office and hurried back over the wall again to hang his poster. It was a fine one of the Duke in *Sands of Iwo Jima*, machine gun in hand, riding on the side of a tank. Lee was especially proud of the flames issuing from the muzzle of the gun, even though he still felt some regret for the Western scene from the previous week's show that he'd had to paint over.

It was only when he was done that he saw the small government notice pasted beside the door to the foyer, and even then he didn't believe it. He had to go back the next night and see the policeman outside. The man stood a little to one side of the main door, looking rather like the guards Lee had seen at the national museum, and every so often stepped forward to wave away people who had come to queue under Lee's poster.

The Savoy cinema had reopened within a couple of weeks and Lee had been briefly rehired, but the new owners, two huge bearded Sikhs whom no one could tell apart, had dispensed with his services when he had begun to experiment with cubism. 'Sorry, sorry,' Lee cried. He claimed his new style was beyond his control. It was a response to the war, he said, but they would hear nothing of it. A new painter — who made every star look like David Niven — was hired.

Lee's family was disgusted with him for losing his job. His father, who ran a machine tool company, had always viewed his son's painting as foolishness, and now it turned out that he could not even make money from it. Once, when his father had asked Lee how he expected to support a family, the young man had said he didn't care about such things. He wanted to be a famous artist.

Everything else would follow. 'Famous for being dirt poor' was all his father had said.

Lee was his father's second son. As a boy he'd been devoted to his older brother. They had built and flown kites together, Lee painting the thin ricepaper and his brother building the intricate bamboo frames. He felt honored to have any part in the kite building and in his childish way decorated the kites as beautifully as he could, although he knew that they were destined for destruction. His brother would coat the strings with glue and roll them in ground glass and then he and the older boys would fly them in fights until one string cut through the other, sending the defeated kite sailing out of sight.

When he was younger, Lee had thought himself well suited to the role of younger brother. He felt no jealousy, only pride, when his father praised his brother's skills, and he was grateful for his brother's occasional compliments. He had only taken the job at the Savoy as a way of supporting studies in draughtsmanship at the technical school — a skill he thought would earn him a useful place at his brother's side for life. But his brother had died of typhoid a year earlier, so fevered at the end that they had poured ice into the bed with him, and Lee, so used to the life of a second son, found himself unable to assume the new role his father wanted of him. In business dealings he was so timid his father grew exasperated. 'You don't strike deals,' he told his son one day. 'They strike you.'

Mr. Lee's business had first blossomed during the Japanese occupation. He'd made a fortune converting cars to run on wood-burning engines when petrol had been rationed. Now once again there was the threat of fuel shortages and Lee was set to useful work gathering a variety of combustible materials. Banana skins were a favoured means of propulsion for his father, as were potato peelings and dung, and the old man delighted in making his son haul the steaming barrels of fuel back and forth across the factory compound. 'At least you'll smell famous,' he called, watching Lee pause to wrap a handkerchief around his nose and mouth.

It was at this time that Lee remembered the Duke showing him an article in a communist paper proving that all the greatest artists had been communists — it was an inevitable result of dialectic materialism, apparently — and he regretted not joining his former employer in the jungle, although in truth it had never occurred to the communists to invite him.

While one half of the family factory was devoted to propulsion experiments, the business in armour-plating cars boomed. Lee's father would lead weekend expeditions into the local countryside to strip the armour off old Japanese tanks and artillery pieces, and these slabs of steel, some up to three inches thick, were bolted to the Austins and Packards of the plantation owners. Lee was taught how to cut the small slits through which the occupants could return fire, and put in charge of painting camouflage. Here, at least, no one complained about his cubist tendencies, and his khaki period would have been a happy one if not for the constant pressure of commerce. On more than one occasion, he was forced to chase after cars leaving the factory to add one final flourish.

By 1951 the family had outfitted nearly every plantation vehicle in the area, and business was beginning to fall off. However, with the introduction of New Villages in that year, Lee's father saw another wonderful opportunity. Under this British initiative, nearly half a million Chinese rubber tappers and their families were to be resettled in purpose-built villages guarded by British troops. The idea was partly to protect communities living on the jungle fringes and partly to deny the communists access to sympathizers in those villages. This was how Lee came to be entrusted with his father's drilling equipment and an ancient wood-burning Austin Princess. By the businessman's reckoning, 500,000 people meant at least 100,000 families, each of whom would need a latrine dug. 'At fifty cents a hole, my son, you might as well be drilling for gold,' he shouted as he waved Lee off.

Lee hated his job, especially when the village children ran after him laughing and shouting 'Mr. Night Soil!' but he did come home with many tales. Once he saw Sardin, the famous Dyak tracker whom the British had brought from Borneo. Sardin was famous for the uncanny jungle skills of his people — he was known to have slept under a string of shrunken heads as a child and for his mouthful of gold teeth. By the time Lee saw him, he had earned nearly enough from the British to have all his own teeth pulled and replaced by gold ones. The whole village crowded around him when he arrived and whenever he smiled broke into wild applause.

Lee, of course, sketched the Dyak and his famous smile, but later that evening, looking at his work again, felt something was missing and drew in the crowd from memory.

Another time, Lee saw General Templer himself. A veteran of three wars, the general had begun his career at eighteen in the First World War, gone on to win the DSO in Palestine, and become the youngest general in the British army in World War II. He was Churchill's personal choice for high commissioner during the Emergency. *The Straits Times* described him on his appointment as an Olympian figure — quite literally, as it turned out. He had been a hurdler in the 1924 games.

When Lee saw him, the general was confronting a group of Chinese Home Guards who had surrendered their weapons without a fight to the communists. 'You're a lot of bastards,' Templer barked. 'But try this again and you'll find out I can be an even bigger one.' Lee, who had learned all his English at the Savoy, understood this kind of language, but he listened politely as the government translator said slowly in Chinese: 'His excellency informs you that he knows none of your mothers or fathers were married when you were born.' The translator paused to let this sink in. 'He does, however, admit that his own mother and father were not married also.'

It was shortly after the mission that killed Lance Corporal Burroughs that the Silver Screen platoon heard a car approaching them along a dusty laterite road. They took cover in the tall lalang at the roadside and on a signal from the Duke opened fire when the lone car drew alongside their position. Sparks and bullets flew off the car's armour, but it did not slacken its pace. Incensed, the Duke leapt from his hiding place and began to pursue it. He knelt in the middle of the road and aimed for the car's rear tires, but although he got off six shots in smart order, he missed each time and the car rolled on toward a small hill in the distance.

The Duke turned away, cursing.

'Wait,' Mr. Cooper shouted. 'He's stopping.'

They all turned to peer at the car on the hillside, which did indeed appear to have pulled up just out of their range. For a full minute they stared hard at the distant car until someone shouted, 'He's not stopping! He can't get over the hill.'

And so it proved. Lee sat at the wheel of the Austin with the car in first and the gas pedal flat to the floor, but still the car, with its armour plating, was too heavy for the wood-burning engine. It could only crawl agonizingly slowly up the gentle slope as he watched the communists overtake him in his mirror. Dazed, his ears still ringing from the clamor of ricochets, he was lucky to hear them when they pushed their guns through the slits in the armour and shouted for him to turn off the engine.

It took Lee a moment to realize whose hands he had fallen into. The Duke's hair, previously immaculately oiled and combed into stiff furrows, was shaved to a close stubble, and there was a gauntness to all the men, even Chen, the former butcher. He allowed the relief to show on his face for a moment and then, thinking better of it, threw himself to his knees to beg for his life.

Mr. Cooper had liked Lee, ever since the night he

had enjoyed, gratis, the favors of a prostitute who thought he really was a film star. Even though the girl in question was known locally as Stupid Suzie, the event had so impressed him that he was inclined to see Lee in an almost magical light. He could see that the Duke was still furious at his failure to hit the tyres of the retreating car. It was a loss of face that he might revenge on Lee, and Mr. Cooper hurriedly pulled him away.

He reminded the Duke that the platoon had recently lost one of their number — an officious young fellow who had been an usher at the Savoy but who'd never looked as imposing with a rifle as he had with a torch. Lee's appearence was an omen, Mr. Cooper said. He would bring them luck. Grudgingly, the Duke said he would give Lee a choice to join them or die.

'What do you say?'

Lee looked up from his knees. 'It's better than drilling latrines,' he said, and Mr. Cooper laughed and clapped him on the back. He was the first new recruit they'd had in two years. They dubbed him Mr. Weissmuller and someone found him a pencil and paper and they made him propaganda officer, responsible for recording their exploits in sketches. He could have a gun, the Duke said, when he'd proved himself reliable.

Lee soon had a chance to record an early success. The next week their platoon encountered a police patrol on the outskirts of a village and exchanged shots before retreating through the rubber trees. In the camp that evening, Lee drew Mr Cooper kneeling behind a tree, sighting along his rifle. 'A souvenir,' Mr. Cooper said when he saw it. 'When we win, I'll have it framed and hung in my shop.' Lee smiled broadly.

The Duke took a long look at the picture and said that they would attack the village again the next day. Mr. Cooper looked up, surprised. 'Don't look so worried,' the Duke said. 'They won't be expecting it.'

He glanced back at the sketch and then at Lee. 'Let's hope you can shoot better than you draw,' he added, but Lee didn't look up.

When they attacked, they were again met with fire from the village, but this time the Duke ordered them not to fall back. The thin rubber trees offered shadows but scant cover. Mr. Chaplin was shot through the neck before Lee's horrified eyes, and they were dangerously pinned down for some minutes until Mr. Murphy outflanked the defenders. They were local police armed with aging rifles and pistols but not the machine guns of the British. Caught in a crossfire, they were forced to retreat, and for the first time in a month the Duke was able to lead his men into the village.

Lee sat to one side sketching the scene while the Duke called the villagers to bring out food. The headman, Mr. Pang, came forward and told him that the police would arrest them if they helped terrorists. The Duke had him tied to a rubber tree at the edge of the plantation, paused a moment, as if listening, and then hacked both his arms off at the elbow with his parang.

'Nothing,' the Duke explained to the other villagers, 'must come between the fighters and the people.' The pencil had broken in Lee's hand, but the Duke lent him a pocket knife and waited patiently while he sharpened it. When he passed it back, Lee hoped he wouldn't notice that his hand was shaking, but the Duke didn't say a word as he snapped the blade away.

Despite temporary successes, morale among the Silver Screen platoon, by this time, was beginning to fail. The British planters around the Ming plantation and then the authorities began to take notice of the fact that the Chinese-owned plantation went unattacked. The rubber tappers of the Ming estate were among the earliest to be resettled in New Villages. At first the men of the Silver Screen platoon joked that they would miss the daughters of the village, and then they began to miss the food. For a time they remained in the vicinity of the New Village — Kampong Coldstream, as it was called, after the British troops who guarded it. Sweethearts and other sympathizers within tried to smuggle them food, but the British were vigilant. They found rice in the frame of a boy's bicycle and even in the brassieres of girls going out to the plantation. 'The best-tasting rice in the world,' Mr. Cooper said ruefully when he told Lee about it.

The platoon began to spend more time hunting through the jungle for food, and their terrorist activity declined, causing dispute among them. The Duke argued that they should attack convoys for food. Mr. Cooper and Mr. Murphy insisted on leading them on long, exhausting foraging missions. Their uniforms, rotted by the damp, fell to rags around them as they gesticulated with one another. Knowing that he was an extra mouth to feed, Lee did not participate in these arguments, but he found himself wishing that they would follow the

Duke's lead. The period before an attack, when the men would lie or crouch motionless for hours beside a road, was ideal for his work, and although the violence repulsed him, he couldn't deny that the sketches he had made of the Duke were some of the best he'd ever done. Even the Duke had commented on the improvement. On the odd occasions when Lee thought back to his paintings for the Savoy, he was gripped with embarrassment for their crude appeal.

In the end the men compromised. They spent a long month hunting for food in the jungle, and when that failed they began to attack villages further afield that had yet to be relocated by the British. In the first, one man clasped his sack of rice to his chest when the Duke tried to pull it from him. He had a pregnant wife to feed, he said. The Duke had him bound and the wife brought out. This was the scene Lee drew: the woman with her belly cut open and the Duke taking the sack of rice from the man's limp hands. For a week afterwards they ate well.

At Mr. Cooper's suggestion they tried to plant gardens in the jungle. The Duke watched the men bending over the rows, placing single grains of rice from their meagre supplies in the soil with their thumb and first finger. 'What are we?' he complained to Lee. 'Are we gardeners?' He was looking through Lee's sketchbook, flicking past the scenes of the men at camp but studying the drawings of their fights. 'Now that's a picture,' he said, jabbing his finger at one, and Lee felt a flush of pride.

The Duke couldn't stop the planting, but he made

the men carry their rifles at all times to remind them they were soldiers. They advanced up the rows bent double, with their weapons slung across their backs, and the only sound was the occasional cursing when someone's gun slipped and cracked him on the elbow.

They had almost finished when they heard the drone of a British plane overhead. 'Come on,' the Duke cried. He pummelled the sore shoulders of the soldiers where they sat and dragged them to their feet. They ran bent over from the stiffness of so much planting, but he pushed them before him.

'What are you doing?' Mr. Cooper called. 'Don't leave the gardens.' He caught the Duke at the edge of the clearing and wrestled him to the ground. For a moment they rolled across the dug earth while the others stooped over them like old men. 'Stop!' Mr. Cooper cried when he could free himself. 'Listen! It's not a bomber, it's only a propaganda plane.' Sure enough, when they listened, they heard only words falling from the sky.

'Comrades,' the tape message began, 'this is a fellow comrade speaking. I know how you are feeling. You are brave fighters, but you are hungry and tired. You are dirty. You are sick. I know it all. I was all of those things, but now I am well. I eat rice twice a day. I bathe every morning.' Lee looked around him and saw the others gazing into the sky, their expressions rapt. 'There is hope, comrades. We are all men. We all make mistakes. I made a mistake and put it right. So can you. It's not hard. Just walk to your nearest police station. There is one not far — '

'You idiots,' the Duke broke in. 'You imbeciles. Do you think those pilots are blind? Do you think they cannot look down into a jungle and see straight lines? There'll be bombers here in an hour.'

'Save yourselves, comrades,' the plane called. 'Save yourselves before it's too late.'

No one moved. Their eyes were fixed on the sky over the clearing. Lee turned, too, and shielded his eyes to look. He could hear the engines of the plane now very clearly, but he could not see it. Suddenly the sky filled with birds.

Not birds, he thought. Paper.

Thousands of sheets of paper were blowing across the treetops and fluttering into the clearing. Men began to rush out from the trees and clutch at them as if they were money. They hopped into the air, catching them in armfuls, stuffing their pockets with them, wadding them up and gripping them in their teeth to free their hands for more. Lee didn't know what they were doing but he watched the others and did as they did.

'Catch me, comrades, catch me,' the plane cried. 'I'm falling. Catch me.'

The Duke snatched at a sheet, missed, and flailed until he caught one. On it was a photograph of three smiling Chinese in neat outfits of shorts and singlets. They sat at a table and were surrounded by British soldiers. One of the soldiers was pouring tea; another held a bottle of rice wine. The table was covered in food. The Duke could clearly make out dishes of chicken's feet, fish-head curry, clay-pot bean curd, prawns with asparagus, char-siu pork, and lemon chicken. The camera had been focused on the food rather than the faces of the three men, but it was still clear that they were smiling. None of them were eating, but each held out before him a porcelain cup. At the top of the sheet were printed only two characters — *yam seng*, 'Cheers.'

'To you, comrades,' said the plane. 'A toast. To you.'

Mr. Cooper was lost in thought. He was remembering the Allied air drops that he had received in the jungle six years before. He was remembering the taste of Bourneville chocolate, how the air seemed filled with its rich sweet scent as the canisters on their parachutes wafted down to them. He didn't see the Duke raise his gun, and he fell to the ground still smiling.

'Now, you dogs,' the Duke cried. 'We haven't much time. Get down on your knees and dig.'

He made them sift through the earth for the rice they had buried, but the only grains they could find were already germinating and not fit to eat. Overhead the voice of the plane receded. It was chanting a list of rewards paid for communists brought in dead or alive. The list was still echoing behind them as the Duke led them away. Any terrorists leading their own comrades out of the jungle were eligible for bounties of $500 or more per head. For platoon leaders the sums mounted dizzyingly into the thousands and tens of thousands. For politburo members, bounties of hundreds of thousands of dollars were rumoured. A last gust of wind high above them carried the voice of the plane back to them once more. 'Think of it, comrades,' it said. 'Just think of it.'

The Duke, in the trees, screamed back, 'Forget Chin

Peng! What about me? What reward for the Duke?' And Lee drew him beating his chest.

Shortly after this the British began sending patrols deeper into the jungle, and it was one of these that the platoon encountered on a humid June day in 1952. They were resting in a small clearing, Lee sketching the men cleaning their weapons, when three British troopers walked in on them. For a moment no one moved. Instinctively, Lee's pencil began the first stroke that would add the newcomers to the scene. The troopers were only the advance guard of their patrol, but despite being outnumbered they reacted first. Mr. Murphy was hit in the opening exchange, but the Duke, with Lee's help, dragged him into the jungle. The Duke was about to return to the fight when the rest of the British entered the clearing and the remaining communists promptly surrendered.

Furious, the Duke watched his men being disarmed, roped together, and then fed. They said little, perhaps aware of their leader's eyes, but they ate eagerly. Lee feared that the Duke would attack the camp, but instead he hoisted Mr. Murphy onto his shoulder. Lee took a last look back at the line of roped men where they lay on the ground, smoking or sleeping, with their hands clasped over their stomachs, and then he was pulled away.

The Duke carried Mr. Murphy for hours, even after he lost consciousness, but he died within the day and they buried him between the roots of a banyan tree. Then for almost two weeks the Duke and Lee wandered through the jungle. They hardly spoke to each other. They fought over what little food they could find. The stock of the Duke's rifle rotted in the damp and broke off when he put it to his shoulder. Lee had had to abandon his sketchbook at the camp, and he was reduced to sketching with a stick in the dust of the trail whenever they took a break. Everything he drew looked like food.

Finally, and quite by chance, they were picked up by another communist patrol. They found that they were almost two hundred miles north of their original base. The communists who found them took them to their commander, who fed them and supplied them with maps and food. He refused, however, to allow them to stay with his group. The Duke nodded sagely, but Lee threw himself to his knees before the commander.

'Please,' he cried. 'I'm a good comrade. Let me join you and be of more use to the party.'

The commander kicked him in the throat and Lee couldn't speak for two days.

The Duke told him he'd been a fool, but gave him a gun at last — an old carbine that the commander had spared them — and taught him to shoot, thinking it might encourage him.

Lee couldn't understand why the commander wouldn't let them join him. After they left the camp, he stumbled through the jungle in a daze, even though the Duke agreed to carry his pack for him. On the second evening, the Duke made him tea and told him that their mission was to return to their former area and reform their unit. Lee could only wail in disbelief.

'We have lost already. There is no one who will join us now.'

The Duke only smiled at him and pulled from his pocket a grubby folded piece of paper. 'Have courage,' he said gently. It was a British leaflet — by this stage of the war over three billion had been dropped on the jungle — but instead of a photograph, a sketch was printed in the centre. It took Lee a moment to recognize it as one of his. The commander of the unit they had encountered had given the leaflet to the Duke. It listed communist leaders and the rewards for their capture. All the politburo members were listed, and just below them the name Ming. The bounty was listed as $250,000. The Duke took the leaflet back and brandished it overhead with a flourish. 'Fame,' he whispered to Lee. 'Fame!' he shouted into the jungle. 'Who could resist joining me? Who could resist the allure of the Silver Screen platoon? We will be irresistible.'

Two days later a train on the Kuala Lumpur–Penang line was flagged down by a ragged figure carrying a gun. Fearing an ambush, although the line had been safe for many months now, the engineer pulled up two hundred yards short of the man. The communist had to shout that he wanted to surrender and he spun round and flung his gun in a high arc into the jungle. The engineer crept closer with the train and then braked again.

'What's that?' he shouted. 'At your feet?'

'He was too heavy,' came the reply. 'It was the only way to claim the reward.'

And Lee held up the severed head of the Duke.

The train took him to a police station in Ipoh, where he had to wait for the constable in charge to come back from his rounds. When the man finally did return, he stood for one long moment looking at Lee and his prize. 'Savages,' he said at last. 'I'm surrounded by savages.' And he handed over a roll of brown paper. 'Wrap that up at once.'

Lee went on to record a number of propaganda messages for the sound planes and trucks of the British. He was also instrumental in setting up a theatre group of surrendered communists who toured New Villages acting out short plays showing the errors of communism. He did not act in these himself but took the role of producer, with particular responsibility for scene painting. These activities were credited with the surrender of almost four hundred more communists, for which Lee enjoyed a share of the reward with his fellow artists. During this time, the British authorities repeatedly warned him against sending any word to his family, but he did pass regular sums of money to his father via policemen he trusted, and for the first time in his life he was truly happy.